REDEMPTION

ALSO BY CHRISTINE BESZE

Destined Trinity

REVENGE SERIES

Revenge

REDEMPTION

REVENGE
BOOK TWO

CHRISTINE BESZE

Redemption
Paperback Edition
Copyright © 2025 by Christine Besze

Love N. Books Press
An Imprint of Wolfpack Publishing
1707 E. Diana Street
Tampa, FL 33610

www.lovenbookspress.com

Cover design by Rachel Chaya Design
Edited by My Brother's Editor

Redemption was originally self-published in 2020 by Christine Besze.

Paperback ISBN 979-8-89567-751-3
Ebook ISBN 979-8-89567-750-6
LCCN 2025946501

For my readers. Thank you so much for all the love and support you have given me through the years.

PLAYLIST

1. Sunday Bloody Sunday by U2
2. The Wish by Madohm
3. Redemption (feat. Lissie) by Skrizzly Adams, Lissie
4. Born Ready by Zayde Wolf
5. Fire Away by Chris Stapleton
6. Simple Man by Shinedown
7. She's a Lady by Big Cock
8. Sail by Devil Driver
9. Ring of Fire by Social Distortion
10. Put the Gun Down by ZZ Ward
11. Pressure by Muse
12. Never Let You Down by Barns Courtney
13. Honky Tonk Women by The Rolling Stones
14. Word Up! by Korn
15. In the Air Tonight by Nonpoint
16. Smooth Criminal by Alien Ant Farm

Use the Spotify link below to read along
with Redemption's playlist:
https://bit.ly/RedemptionPlaylist

REDEMPTION

REDEMPTION

PROLOGUE
KELSEY

I'm running through the front door of my house in a fog. My brain is still trying to make sense of what just happened tonight. There was so much blood, but she's going to be okay. That's all that matters. What hurts the most in all of this is Axel's betrayal. He lied to me from the time I laid eyes on him. Broke my heart and shattered it into a million pieces.

"Mom! Dad!" I continue on through the house into the living room where I find my parents sitting down with a cup of tea.

"What is it? What's wrong?" My dad's eyebrows draw together as he sets his cup down on the coffee table.

They take one look at my appearance, and my mother gasps. Charlee's blood still coats my clothes and hands. My face throbs, and I'm sure there are some big bruises forming. That's the least of my problems right now.

"What happened to ye?" Her Irish accent has faded over time, but it still slips out when she's stressed, much to my father's disapproval.

"I...Charlee—" My throat closes up as it becomes impossible to form words. "I need to get out of here. Disappear for a while. Please." I've never asked my parents for anything like this before, but I know they have the resources to make it happen. And I need to be somewhere where I can clear my head. Far away from a blue-eyed bastard whose dimples make me weak in the knees. The bastard who's a silver-tongued snake.

My dad stares at me for a minute before nodding his head. "I'll take care of it. You get cleaned up and meet me in my office."

"Thank you." With that, I run off to shower and pack my things.

Minutes later, I'm standing in my dad's office with a brand-new pair of brown cowgirl boots on and a new identity in hand.

Tonight's the night Kelsey Loren dies and Lorelei Smith is born.

1

KELSEY

LONG BEACH, CALIFORNIA—TWO YEARS
LATER...

The toes of my cowgirl boots crunch under the mounds of peanut shells that litter the concrete floor and "Meant to Be" by Bebe Rexha & Florida Georgia Line blares through the system's speakers as I head off to take the order of my next table.

Gilley's is one of the few restaurants that still thrives on this deserted block. Cowboy hats line the walls, and framed pictures of famous Western actors are hung above each booth. It's a bit dated inside with a home-town country feel, and I love it. It's a piece of history that's been here for years. The musty smell seeping through the wood-paneled walls is proof of that.

Two years of this and nothing changes. I'm twenty-three years old, and all I do is eat, work, sleep, repeat. It's a steady routine. Something I never thought I'd want. Something I never thought I'd even like.

Here, things are different. No one knows who I am. No one knows what I've been through. It's safe. Safe is good, but sometimes it's boring as fuck.

"How's it going, Lorelei? You look tired as hell, dude." Natalie swings her hips up to the counter and whips her blonde head around to face me. She's the only "friend" I've really managed to make out here. The rest are just acquaintances, nothing more. As far as dating goes, that's something I'm steering far, far away from. Ever since a blue-eyed, lying asshole with dimples and a smooth Southern accent that could set panties on fire ruined my life, I've stayed clear of anything with a dick.

"Exhausted is more like it." I laugh as I slap the ticket order into the metal clip and spin the wheel around.

"A bunch of us are heading down to the beach tomorrow. You should come." Her brown eyes glance up at me with what appears to be hope.

"I don't know." Hesitation has become a natural occurrence for me, and I hate it. I used to be the one planning all the spontaneous trips for Charlee and me. Now, I'm the one having to be dragged out to have a good time. If only she could see me now.

My heart hurts at the thought of my best friend. On the many nights I've spent crying myself to sleep, I've often wondered how she's doing. I could have asked my dad, but that would only make my pain so much worse. Sometimes, it is better not to know that life goes on without you.

"Come on. You'll have fun." Natalie hip checks me out of my inner thoughts.

"Bonfires and beer? Count me in." I smile, forcing

some of the old Kelsey to shine through, but inside, I feel a piece of me is still missing.

"That's the spirit." She slaps me on the shoulder and heads off to check on her tables.

I do the same, and before long Gilley's is packed. I'm kept so busy that I don't have time to dwell on the ghosts of my past or the shit show that has become my life.

When my shift finally ends, I'm about dead on my feet. I toss my apron on a hook in the back and head out the door. The salty air blows across my skin, causing goose bumps to arise. It's a cool summer night, and I'm kicking myself for forgetting a damn sweater. My arms fold over across my chest in a sad attempt to keep warm.

Natalie's invite rolls around inside my head the entire five-minute walk from Gilley's to my set of apartments. I'm so tired of breathing but not really living.

Screams of laughter from the beach skate across the night sky, hitting me in the stomach with envy. I contemplate going back to my cramped apartment alone to pass out, but that's what Lorelei would do. Kelsey wants to live—to feel the ocean dance along her skin and take chances.

Mind made up, I bypass the alley to my apartment and head toward the beach. My apartment may be a shithole, but its quick access to the beach is a fancy perk I'm appreciative of right now.

Sand kicks up with each step, coating my boots. The palms of my hands sweat, but I keep moving forward. I can do this. I *need* to do this.

Flames flicker higher inside the fire pit the closer to the group I get. A few people give me a nod as I search for a certain familiar face. Lucky for me, I don't have to wait long before I see a flash of blond rushing straight toward me.

"You made it." Natalie pushes up on her toes to wrap her arms around me in a hug. I bend down and meet her halfway. The glazed-over look in her eyes tells me she's been having fun for a while. "You need a drink."

"I do." I exhale a shaky laugh and follow her toward another small group of guys that are hovering around a red ice chest.

"Guys, this is Lorelei." She waves her hand back and forth between myself and the group. "Lorelei, that's Alan, Mark, and Steven." A long pink fingernail points from the blond to the two brunettes.

"Hi." I clear my throat and do a small wave back like the dork I am.

All three of them return my lame gesture with a chin lift, and we stand in awkward silence for a few seconds. It's almost like high school all over again.

Natalie hands me a bottle of beer, giving me something to do with my hands. I waste no time cracking that sucker open and let the crisp fluid cool my overheated body. I'm so out of practice with peopling that I suck at it. I swallow so fast I damn near choke.

"Whoa, you might want to slow down on that." Alan laughs and runs his fingers through his blonde hair and breaks away from his friends. He's wearing a pair of black board shorts and a white puka shell necklace that I'm pretty sure went out of style in the '90s, but it's his shoes that have me second-guessing this guy. *Who wears penny loafers to the beach?*

"Thanks." I wipe the back of my hand over my mouth and try to ignore the fact that I just made an ass out of myself. If my lack of etiquette is a turnoff, he isn't letting on because he's still closing the distance between us.

"So." He shoves his hands in his pockets and stares down at his feet a bit before his brown eyes lift up and meet mine. "What would it take for you to consider going out with me tomorrow night?"

"You don't waste any time, do you?" I laugh at my own joke, but inside I'm dying.

"Not when I see something I want." His brown eyes glisten, but they are nothing like the blue ocean I'm used to staring into.

At that moment, the breeze picks up, and the familiar smell of cedarwood hits me. My eyes flicker to the parking lot a few times, but come up empty. It doesn't stop the uneasiness swirling in the pit of my stomach. I can't help but feel like I'm being watched, but that's stupid. No one knows where I am. Hell, no one even knows who I really am.

"Everything okay, Lorelei?" Alan asks, bringing me back to the present.

"Yup. Totally fine." I snap my attention back to him and let my own stupidity fade away.

"About tomorrow night?" He tilts his head to the side and waits for my answer.

My eyes do a head-to-toe inspection of him. Everything about him screams safe. His smile seems so clean-cut. So cookie cutter. So the opposite of a dark-haired demon that broke my heart. And maybe that's what I need?

"Sure. I'd love to go out with you tomorrow night."

"Awesome." His lips spread into a wide smile showing off his over-bleached teeth as he leans in and brushes away a stray strand of hair from my cheek.

I force out a smile, ignoring the knot forming in the pit of my stomach, and toss back more of my beer in a silent toast. Things are only going to change if I take the initiative, and that's exactly what I'm going to do. Come tomorrow, Lorelei Kahlo will be one step closer to melting into what's left of Kelsey Loren.

2

AXEL

I light up a cigarette and toss the rest of the pack on top of my dash before going back to doing the same thing I have for the past few nights from my truck—watch. Watch the way her tan legs flex against the force of the sand when she walks. Watch the way her long red hair blows in the wind like a halo of fire around her.

Time has done her body good. Curves in all the right places. Tits that I know all too well will fill my hands. And an ass that's ripe for the squeezing. My teeth dig into my bottom lip, and my jeans become tighter as I continue to stare like a starved man dying of a thirst only she can quench.

The second I caught a glimpse of that auburn hair through the diner window the other night, I knew it was her. My hands itch to wrap those same strands around my fist and pull her back against me as I fuck her from behind. Two years is a fucking long time to go without her, and my body's ready to claim her once again. My dick twitches in agreement.

Seeing her stand with that group, looking so lost and out of place, only deepens my need. The dickweed she's talking to doesn't help the situation either. He looks like a walking Abercrombie & Fitch ad and is getting much too close for my liking. I squeeze the grip of the steering wheel tighter until I can hear the plastic buckle from the pressure.

When he leans in and pulls a strand of hair from her face, letting his fingers linger on her skin too long, all bets are off. I have my hand on the door handle, ready to go whoop some Yankee ass, when the passenger-side door of my truck is ripped open and slammed back shut.

"What the hell, man? Take it easy. Willie Mae ain't no new truck. She's fragile." I damn near drop my cigarette and burn my dick off as I snap my head in his direction.

"She's a damn truck, Ax." Zane gives me a look before relaxing against the black vinyl. He shakes his head at me, causing the man bun on top of his head to move like dead weight. Tattoos snake up his right arm and disappear underneath his black T-shirt. He doesn't nearly have enough ink like Asher or myself, but even without it, he looks so much like our oldest brother right now it's scary. He's even filled out more muscle wise to match Asher. I'm not far behind them, but at least my biceps don't get in the way when I answer my phone.

"No, she ain't. This old girl is more than that, and you know it." I pat the top of my dashboard and console Willie Mae. She's more than just a truck to me. Neither one of my brothers can understand the love a man has for his vehicle, but I'll be damned if they diss my girl. "Someone's in a bitch mood. You need to get laid, man."

He rolls his eyes and adjusts the knot of dark hair on top of his head. I don't know why he doesn't cut that shit off already and call it a day. "You mention how much you got laid in here one more time and I'm kicking your ass."

"Fine." I inhale another hit off my cigarette and blow the smoke in his direction. "Why are you here?"

He tilts his head, studying me a minute before he speaks. "Had a feeling you might do something stupid."

"Well, you can go run back to big brother and let Asher know I got my shit together." I wave my hand toward the door. The sooner he gets out of here, the sooner I can go get my woman and drag her ass back home.

His blue eyes that are the same damn color as mine glance toward the direction of the group before coming back to me. I know what he sees as soon as he opens his damn mouth. "Right."

"Like I said. I got it handled." I shrug off his stare and flick the ash of my cigarette out the small crack of my window.

"Really?" He cocks a dark eyebrow as he flicks his chin between me and back toward the beach. "So, you weren't about to get out of the truck and go pounce on that preppy prick for putting the moves on your woman?"

"Nooooo." I shake my head back and do my best to keep my face blank.

"Bullshit." He stares me down, seeing right through my ass. I don't even know why I try. He's like a fucking lie detector. All three of us are, really, but Asher would just call me out for being stupid and storm off. Not Zane. No, he always wants to go all Dr. Phil on your ass and talk shit out. Asher does too, but with his fists. That thought has me suddenly wondering which one would be the less painful option right about now.

"Fine." I shrug. "I may have wanted to show him what happens when you mess with a Southern boy's woman." I take another drag off my cigarette and take my time exhaling. The longer I take, the more I'm sure it irritates the shit out of him, and that makes me smile on the inside.

"What was your plan after that? Hogtie her ass up and toss her in the back seat?" He shakes his head at me and steals a smoke from my pack.

"I mean..." Images of her bound and gagged flood my head, sending all of the blood straight to my dick. I shift against the seat to avoid the roughness of my jeans from cutting off the circulation to my balls and fight the urge to jump from this truck and throw her ass over my shoulder so I can do just that.

"Jesus, Ax. Stop thinking with your dick for once." He smacks me on the back of the head before lighting up his cigarette, killing thoughts of Kelsey and my hard-on all in one go. "We have to be discreet about this. All of our asses are on the line with this. You fuck it up, and we won't get any more high-profile clients."

"I fucking know that, Z." My body tenses as he scolds me like I'm a damn kid.

He must sense I'm close to losing it because he eases up. "Look, her dad wants her brought back home quietly, which means we need to play this smart. Sleep on it, and we'll figure out a plan of attack for tomorrow night."

My thumb rubs along my bottom lip as I do my best to calm my rising temper and let his words roll off my back. "I know what her dad wants." Too bad I don't give a shit. My Wildcat is coming back home, but with me where she belongs. I just need to convince her of that without having her scratch my eyes out first.

3
KELSEY

"Freaks" by Timmy Trumpet and Savage pumps through the speakers as I and a couple of friends from art class tear it up on the dance floor. A purple haze of light bounces off the black floors as we lose ourselves in the killer beat. Cages hang from the ceiling with a dancer inside each one. Their black bikinis and matching thigh-high boots glow against the purple lighting. The black and purple color scheme is continued throughout the club.

Beads of sweat drip down my back and between my breasts, but I don't stop. There's nothing more freeing than dancing. After a few more songs, my body is screaming for some hydration. I signal to my friends with my finger that I'll be back and spin on my green heels toward the bar.

The same black and purple theme is continued over here with purple lighting accenting the endless bottles of liquor and a black countertop. People crowd around the small space, but I manage to shove my way through and order a water. I'm leaning against the counter when I feel someone staring at me. I twist to the side and tilt my head back, taking in the fine specimen before me. He towers over me, making my five-foot-six frame seem tiny in comparison. Tattooed arms connected to a rock-hard chest give way to a pair of the most gorgeous blue eyes I've ever seen and a head full of trimmed brown hair. A cigarette is pinched between his fingers as the plumes of smoke dance around the air between us.

"It's not polite to stare." I arch an eyebrow at him.

"That right?" His lips spread into a wide smile, revealing a deep set of dimples. The rest of him is just as delicious looking. Muscles that are on display through his tight green T-shirt that lead to an impressive pair of jean-clad thighs, but what really does it for me is the faded cowboy boots.

"Yup." I emphasize the P at the end with a loud pop, drawing his eyes to my lips.

"I'd say I'm sorry about that, Wildcat, but I'm not. You're fucking gorgeous." His Southern accent only adds to his hotness.

"Wildcat?" I tilt my head to the side and purse my lips.

"You're upfront and won't hesitate to bring out your claws." All the blood rushes to my face at his words and I open my mouth to tell him off, but he winks. "And that's a compliment, Red."

"I'm Kelsey." I hold my hand out, showing off the good manners that my parents ingrained in me—the only thing I've listened to them on.

"Shawn." He takes my hand in his and brings it to his lips in a soft kiss. The warmth of his skin against mine causes a ripple of shivers to race through me.

Little did I know that that night would change my life so drastically. All because I couldn't resist a pair of baby blue eyes and those damn dimples. Dimples that landed me in my current situation.

After another long shift, I power walked to shower and wash the smell of grease and sweat off me. I'm still not too sure about this guy Alan, but at least I'm getting myself out there. This is the first step in getting my life back.

I'm showered and dressed in a white summer dress that I paired with my favorite pair of tan cowgirl boots when the doorbell rings.

The second I open it, my heart drops. My whole world is knocked on its ass as I glare up at all six-foot-one of him. This can't be happening. "What the fuck?"

"Hello, Wildcat." His brown hair is a bit longer than the last time I saw him, but those damn dimples are just as deep as the first time I met him. It takes a hell of a lot for me to keep focused, but I manage. He's not conning me—not again.

I move to slam the door in his face, but I'm not fast enough, and he manages to slip a foot inside. He uses his muscular weight to force the door open further, pushing his way inside. I know I'm in trouble the second he shuts the door and twists the lock.

Instinct has me wanting to run, but I stand my ground. He's not going to intimidate me into being a coward. I've done enough of that all on my own the past two years. I stay where I am, cross my arms over my chest, and give him my best death glare. At least if I'm angry, I can't pay too much attention to how good he looks in his black jeans and navy T-shirt that molds against all of his muscles like a second skin.

As always, he ignores my bitchy attitude and goes about his business. His eyes do a quick inventory of my tiny apartment before settling on my small pink couch. "Nice place. May want to rethink that couch though, Wildcat." He opens his mouth to say something else, but my patience is wearing thin, and I don't let him.

"Cut the shit, Axel. What the hell are you doing here?" A sigh escapes me as I wait for him to answer.

"Missed you too." He strolls around like he owns the place and makes himself at home by plopping down on my couch. I don't miss the way his massive form overpowers the tiny wooden frame. "I must admit, this is ugly as fuck, but it's pretty comfy." His large hand pats the bottom cushion.

I do my best to ignore those hands or how good they felt on my body and stay focused on the flood of emotions coursing through me. "That wasn't an invitation, asshole."

He leans back further against the couch and rests one arm on top of the couch as his eyes do a head-to-toe inspection of me. "Looking good. Where you goin' all dressed up like that, Wildcat?"

"Not that it's any of your business, but I have a date." His whole body tenses at those words, but since I'm on a roll, I keep going as I walk over and open the door. One hand grips the knob as I wave for him to get out with the other. "Which means you need to leave. I'd say it was good to see you, but we both know that's a load of crap."

He eyes me for a minute, and I wait for him to lose

his shit, but I should know better. This man never does what I expect. "He's not coming."

"What do you mean he's not coming?" My hand squeezes tighter around the metal knob to keep me in place. Otherwise, he'd have my boot up his ass.

"You know, sugar in the gas tank is a bitch to get out. Or so I hear."

"What the hell, Axel?" I cannot believe him.

The edges of his mouth curl up into a smile that makes his blue eyes light up. "A fucking puka shell necklace, really, Wildcat?"

It takes a second for his words to register before my emotions get the best of me. I slam the door shut and stomp over to where he's sitting until the tips of my boots come into contact with his. That's as close as I'm allowing us to get. "Have you been stalking me?"

"It's not stalking to watch out for what belongs to me." His head tilts up to meet my gaze.

"Says every stalker out there." I roll my eyes toward the ceiling. "And I don't belong to you."

"You do." He shrugs a shoulder at me but doesn't move from his position otherwise. "Pack a bag, Red. It's time to come home."

"No way. I'm not going anywhere with you." I take a couple of steps back, needing a bit of distance from him. He's too much sometimes.

"That's the only time I'll ask nicely." He sits up and shifts his body weight forward like he's ready to stand but hangs his hands between his legs.

"Fuck you!" My hands clench into fists at my sides.

"Maybe later. Right now, we're pressed for time." He shrugs but doesn't take his eyes off of me.

"Axel. Or is it Shawn? You lying asshat." I shake my head so hard I'm surprised that I don't end up with whiplash.

"I didn't technically lie. That is my middle name." He slowly stands to his feet and tilts his head to the side.

"Glad you think you're funny, but I'm still not coming back with you."

"You don't have a choice in the matter, *Kelsey*." The way he says my name should serve as enough of a warning, but as usual I let my mouth run off without thinking.

My whole body stiffens at the underlying threat those words hold. "You bet your ass I do."

"You don't. Everyone wants you back home." He rubs his thumb along his bottom lip as he watches me. "Me, your parents, Charlee."

A slight pang hits my chest at the mention of my best friend's name, but I can't let him drag me back there. "This is ridiculous. Leave right now, or I'm calling the police." I storm over to my kitchenette and grab my cell off the counter. "I'm not kidding, Axel. This is your one and only warning."

I expect him to freak out or yell, but he doesn't. He stands there staring at me with something working behind his eyes, causing my heart to pound against my chest with each second that ticks by. His silence is almost worse than his smart mouth.

"Time's up." I glance down and start dialing, but I only get the first number punched in before the phone is taken out of my hand, and I'm thrown over his shoulder like a sack of potatoes.

"I can see some things haven't changed." He laughs

and spanks me on the ass as he stomps into my room. His hands dig into my thighs as he slides me down his body until I'm standing upright.

The second my feet hit the floor, I attempt to make a run for it, but I don't even get a step in before I feel the bite of cold metal against my wrist.

"What the fuck?" I jerk my arm and see his at the same time. "You just handcuffed me to you."

"You never complained before. In fact, I remember you asking me to—"

My free hand covers his mouth as heat floods my face. "Don't even say it."

He smiles against my hand, and then I feel something warm and wet tickle my palm.

"Gross." My nose wrinkles as I wipe my hand on the bottom of my dress. "I can't believe you just licked me."

"Won't be the last time either." He winks and goes back to packing my clothes with one arm. I don't have much, so he's done in a matter of minutes and tosses the bag over his shoulder. He tugs me along toward the door, with me fighting against him the whole way.

"I told you I'm not going back." I dig my heels into the floor and yank on the cuffs once more, but he nudges me into his chest with a slight jerk of his arm and presses his lips against mine.

My mouth gasps open at the sudden movement, and he takes full advantage. His tongue slips inside, controlling me from the inside out. A groan escapes me, and just when I'm about to pull him in for more, he breaks it.

"We can fight about this inside, Willie Mae." He leads me out the door, lost in a lust-filled haze, and doesn't stop until we reach the bottom of the stairs, near the parking lot.

We only make it a few steps after that when there's a giant explosion. One minute I'm on my feet, and the next, I'm being pinned to the ground by a pair of familiar strong arms. "Motherfuckers blew up my truck!"

4

AXEL

A ball of fire lights up the night sky as I drop Kelsey's bag, grab her by the arm, and dive behind some bushes for safety. My arms cradle her as close to me as I can to keep her from taking the brunt of my weight and crushing her. Not an easy thing to do as we're still cuffed together. Maybe that wasn't my smartest idea given our current situation, but it was the only way I could make her come with me. Not to mention my dick likes this new position a hell of a lot, despite the circumstances. Her mango scent isn't helping matters. The fruity shit that is unique only to her has my balls tightening and aching for her.

Then my eyes take in the damage in front of us, and it's like a splash of ice water on my dick. I see red. Willie Mae is in a million fiery pieces sprawled throughout the darkened parking lot. I'm about to bust someone's ass as I watch my precious truck being blown to fucking pieces, but then the bullets start flying. One hits the ground damn near next to Kelsey's head, causing her to flinch in my arms.

"Shit." My head snaps around as I do a quick scan of our surroundings. The building's piss-poor lights give way to a few small potted plants and the stairs where we came from. Other than that, there's nothing else for us to use as cover. We're fucked if we stay where we are. "Wildcat, I need you to do something for me."

"What?" Her voice comes out a quiet and shaky mess, and tears glisten her blue eyes, hitting me square in the chest. It kills me to see her like this, and that pisses me off all over again. It makes me want to rip their intestines out through their fucking throats for each droplet that falls down her perfect face. Something I'll enjoy doing the first chance I get, but right now I have more important things to handle. I suck down my rage and focus on getting us out of this alive.

"We need to move. We're sitting ducks right now. When I tell you to, I need you to run as fast as those gorgeous legs can carry you that way." I jerk my head to the small opening on the right of us. "Can you do that for me?"

She nods, but her auburn eyebrows pinch together. "What about you?"

I pull out my Glock and make sure there's one in the chamber before glancing up at her and holding up our linked hands. "I'll be right behind you, just don't slip on the wet asphalt, or we'll both be fucked."

After a few seconds pass, the firing finally stops, meaning they have to reload, and I don't waste another second. I pull Kelsey to her feet and gently shove her toward the open back of the building with me right behind. "Now, Wildcat."

My cuffed hand intertwines with hers as I use my body as a shield and keep firing with my right one until we're tucked safely behind the building. The salty sea air has me sweating like a hog on a spit, but we keep moving. Building after building, we weave our way through as best as the shitty lights will allow, with heavy footsteps pounding the pavement right behind us.

On our last turn, we wind up in a darkened alley that opens up onto a street at the end. We're almost to the end of the building, which means we'll lose our only source of protection. I need to think of something fast, or else it's open season on our asses.

A flash of green out of the corner of my eye catches my attention under the faded streetlight. Without giving it a second thought, I shove us behind the dumpster. The putrid smell of trash and who knows what else has Kelsey fighting her gag reflex. Lucky for me, I've been in worse situations overseas and can stomach much more than this nasty shit.

Footsteps pound against the wet asphalt closer to where we're hiding, and I slide us deeper into the building until our bodies are tucked tightly inside the small crevice between the wall and the dumpster.

The figures step into the light, and I do a quick inventory of what I'm up against. There are only two of them, but I get the feeling the rest are waiting back at her apartment and will come charging over the second we're found. The younger one is wearing dress slacks with suspenders, while the older, bald one of the pair appears to be an annoying ass mouth breather that I can hear hyperventilating from here.

"Ye feckin' idiot. The girl needs to be brought in alive without a scratch on her." He smacks the younger one across the back of the head so hard he stumbles back a few steps. There's no missing their Irish accents, and that's information that I file away inside my head for later.

Kelsey groans at that. I press her up against the brick wall and put my hand over her mouth to keep them from hearing her. If they do, we're fucked. The metal of the cuff digs into my skin, but I ignore the slight bite of pain and focus on them.

"Sorry, Carrick." His voice comes out a bit high-pitched. Christ, he sounds like he's still a fucking kid.

"It's fine, lad. Let's find her and get out of here." He waves the kid off as they start pulling on the doors that line the brick buildings. One by one they yank on the locked doors, creeping closer to where we're hiding.

Kelsey jerks against my hold, and I tighten my hand over her mouth to keep her quiet. I feel her heart pounding against her chest as she fights to control her trembling body. My focus is split on keeping her quiet and the dicks a few feet in front of us. I need to try to form some sort of plan, but my options are slim. We're outnumbered and outgunned, which I could handle if it was just my ass on the line and not cuffed to her, but it's not, and no way am I risking her ending up with a bullet in her gorgeous body.

The bald one called "Carrick" gets a call and shouts over his shoulder to the kid before he walks off toward the apartments. The younger one hangs back, looking around and heading straight for the dumpster that's our shelter. I aim my gun at his head, ready to pull the trigger when a rumble of an engine catches my attention.

A lifted black truck guns it down the alley, never

slowing down. The front bumper nails the dipshit in his shoulder, and he's knocked back a good distance, sliding against the asphalt.

The window rolls down, and I about choke out a sigh of relief. Zane's in the driver's seat with a cigarette hanging from his mouth, looking like he's on a late-night drive, and I've never been happier to see the fucker's bearded face in my life.

"Hop in." He jerks his head to the cab of the truck.

I release Kelsey and slide into the back seat, knowing she'll have no choice but to follow since we're stuck together. She slides in against my side but doesn't even put up a fight. Since we ran through a hail of bullets, she's been as silent as a mouse. And that worries me. My Wildcat is never quiet.

In a moment of weakness, I pull out the key with my free hand and bring her wrist into my lap. The movement causes the metal of the cuffs to clank together, catching Zane's attention, but I ignore him and continue what I'm doing. The cuff springs free with a small click, but Kelsey doesn't even move. Her hand stays limp on my thigh. I wrap my arm around her shoulder and pull her closer to my side. It's like she's here, but she's not really here with us.

The sound of Zane clearing his throat has my eyes darting up to meet his through the rearview mirror. He cocks a dark eyebrow at me, but I shake my head, letting him know to drop it. There's no way in hell I'm explaining why we were cuffed together. With a small shrug, he goes back to paying attention to the road, but I know him. I'll be hearing about it later.

We drive a few minutes in stifled silence until Zane breaks it. "Where's Willie Mae?"

"She blew up." My lips flatten into a tight line as my foot taps against the black carpet.

"Blew up?" He damn near chokes on his cigarette, sending sparks flickering toward his beard.

I clear my throat a few times before giving him a one-word answer. The wound is still too fresh to do much else. "Yup."

Zane's blue eyes take turns going from the road to my reflection in the mirror. He doesn't open his mouth, but I know he wants to. After a couple more times of this, my agitation hits its peak.

"Don't even say it." I shift against the black leather seats and squeeze Kelsey's side a bit tighter. She flinches but doesn't make a move otherwise. I'm not sure if that's a good sign or not.

"Wasn't gonna." He shrugs and blows a puff of smoke out the open window.

"Right." The phone in my back pocket starts ringing, and as soon as I lay eyes on the caller ID, my whole body tenses. "Shit."

"You might want to answer that." Zane messes with the pile of hair on top of his head, and I want to smack that mop, but I refrain.

"Nah, I'm good." I glare at my brother through the rearview mirror as I shut my phone off and shove it into my back pocket.

Zane takes a sharp turn onto the freeway but doesn't bring up the phone call I'm doing everything in my power to avoid. I stare out the window, letting the shit that happened in the last fifteen minutes roll through my head. Probably wasn't the best idea to do that, but I'm not spending the long trip we have ahead of us with

Asher chewing my ass out. I need to focus on my Wildcat and who the hell was shooting at her.

Not to mention those fuckers blew up Willie Mae, and for that alone, I'll have their balls in a vise.

5
KELSEY

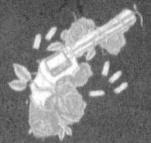

T he engine vibrates through my body, but it does little to calm the storm that's attempting to swallow me up from the inside. Images of what happened are stuck on repeat in my head no matter how hard I try to block them out. The confines of my dress feel like a noose squeezing my insides like a vise as the smell of smoke fills the air. Conversation is happening around me, but it's a mass of white noise. A slight sting of pain from the side of my leg slowly seeps through, but it's not enough to shake me out of it.

The only thing keeping me from crawling out of my skin and shaking like a leaf is the warmth of the body next to me. It's the same one that I've spent the last two years hiding from, and for good reason. He's been back in my life less than an hour, and already things are back to the same crazy shit they were before I skipped town. Axel's dangerous to me for so many reasons. Reasons he's just proved to me, yet again.

That's enough to knock me out of my comatose state and get myself together. I jerk out of his arms, sending him a glare. Most of his face is hidden in shadow, but the few lights from the city cast a slight glow as we pass them, giving me glimpses of his strained features.

"What the hell is going on? Who were those guys? Why were they shooting at us?" Once I open my mouth, there's no stopping the rapid fire of questions that pour out of it. It's a serious case of verbal diarrhea that I can't control, not that I want to.

"I don't know." A muscle in his cheek jumps as his lips press together in a tight line. Lips that I'm all too familiar with. Ones that are soft and magical to the touch as they work you into several orgasms.

I cross my legs and ignore the warmth pooling in my core. My body may have a mind of its own, but I force myself to think with my big girl head. I shake myself out of the past and all of the memories that have kept me up many nights before pointing my finger in his face. "Bullshit, you don't. Things were fine until you showed up on my doorstep, and now we're on the run and driving to who the hell knows where." My hand balls up into a tight fist and slams against the side of my leg. I ignore the slight sting and focus on the source of all my pain.

Through the dark, I can feel his blue gaze harden on mine. "You heard them in the alley, Wildcat. They weren't after me. It's you they want."

My heart pounds against my chest as his words sink in. I heard what they said, but I still refuse to believe that he could be right. "You're lying." He has to be. He better be. It's the only thing that makes sense.

"That's not true, and—" He leans in closer until the heat of his breath blows across my cheek, sending the faintest hint of tobacco my way. The familiar scent sends a trail of shivers through me. "—deep down, you know it." He reaches up and cups the side of my face. Our eyes lock through the dark cab of the truck, and everything else fades away. The fingers of his right hand glide against my cheek in small, steady strokes. They're the perfect mixture of warmth and roughness.

All of the air in the cab becomes stifled with our lust. His head descends further, but before he can press his lips to mine, the ringing of a cell phone has us freezing and reminding us that we are not alone.

"Yeah?" Zane's deep voice echoes through the small space like a bomb.

The interruption is enough to have me come back to my senses. I break our connection and sit back against my side of the truck far enough away that I can think with a clear head. My hands run along the edge of my dress as my teeth begin to chatter from the loss of his warmth.

"Don't be so stubborn." Axel wraps his arm around my shoulders and pulls me in tight against his side once again. The familiar scent of cedarwood and tobacco surrounds me. It's one that used to make my toes curl, and judging by the butterflies swirling inside my stomach, not much has changed.

"Thanks." I should have known he would notice my chattering teeth. Nothing gets past him.

He leans in and kisses the side of my head. My heart stutters at the contact. Memories of how sweet he can be are wreaking havoc on both my body and my brain.

I glance up into the rearview mirror to find Zane's stare directed at me with a cigarette hanging out of the corner of his mouth, and a scorching heat spreads across my cheeks. A part of me feels embarrassed that we just aired our business in front of him, but another is too tired to care.

"Ash." Zane's voice comes out smooth and calm, but Axel's body goes rigid next to me at the mention of his older brother's name, and my own stomach drops to the floor.

His name causes a tightness in my chest. It's a cold reminder of what I left behind—Charlee. A lump forms in my throat at the thought of her. That's just another reason I'm not ready to return to Georgia. It might make me a coward, but I'm not ready to see the hurt on her face.

"I'll let him know. Later." Zane hangs up and lets a beat of silence pass by before breaking it. "You're welcome."

"Don't remember saying thank you." Axel leans an elbow against the door of his truck and shakes his head.

"You will when we get home." Zane's words are ominous, but it's the last one that has me sitting up ramrod straight.

"Oh no. I told you I'm not going back there. Let me out of this truck right fucking now!" I attempt to twist out of Axel's hold, but his grip on me tightens.

I meet Zane's blank stare through the rearview mirror and give him my best intimidating glare. I've only met him once, and it was the night I try not to remember, but it was enough to know he's harboring secrets of his own. That gives me a sliver of hope he might take pity on me, but that's my first mistake. He cocks an eyebrow at me, not threatened in the least by my attitude. Other than that, he doesn't say a word.

My nostrils flare as I slump back against the seat, breaking Axel's hold on me, and cross my arms over my chest. "We'll see about that," I mumble to myself as I stare out the window, doing my best to ignore the two of them.

Axel leans in closer until I feel the warmth of his lips brushing against the shell of my ear, and he whispers just loud enough for me to hear, "Don't test me, Wildcat. Or I'll spank that gorgeous ass of yours until it's as red as your hair."

A gasp escapes me, but I cover it up and press my lips together into a firm line to keep from adding fuel to the fire. If there's one thing my dad taught me, it's to pick your battles wisely. Not to mention, they have another thing coming if they think they can tell me what to do.

The rest of the drive is done in silence. There's no use arguing with either one of them. They're as stubborn as I am. I'll just have to bide my time and wait for the right moment to escape. And escape, I will.

6

KELSEY

After the shootout at my apartment, the boys were itching to put as many miles between us and California as possible. We make it all the way to Albuquerque, only stopping for gas, snacks, and bathroom breaks in between.

At the first stop, I attempted to escape, but Axel put an end to that idea real quick. I swear the bastard has ninja-like reflexes. He made it clear he isn't letting me out of his sight. I thought he was full of shit until he stood outside the bathroom door. A few choice words fell out of my mouth, but the fucker just laughed and closed the door in my face. Which is why I'm still staring out the window like it's the most fascinating thing I've ever seen hours later. I've watched the sun rise and set, all while ignoring the body heat that's occupying the space next to me.

I'm jerked out of my thoughts when Zane pulls off into an empty motel parking lot and kills the engine in a spot right near the door. He stubs the butt of his cigarette out in the ashtray before glancing over his shoulder at the two of us with a cocked eyebrow. "I'll go check us in." The truck door slams, and he heads off to the front office without sparing us a second glance.

Silence stretches between us like a rubber band that's ready to snap back in our faces at any moment, but I'll be damned if I'm going to be the first one to break.

A few more beats pass, but still, neither of us makes a move to put an end to it. Then, the warmth of a hand clamps down on my upper thigh and squeezes. My whole body tenses from the sudden contact. It takes everything in me not to turn and spew my wrath in his face, but part of me thinks that's what he wants, so I stay perfectly still and keep my focus locked on a piece of trash floating underneath the lights in the desolate parking lot.

Whiskers tickle against the shell of my ear as soft lips move against my skin. "You can be pissed at me all you want, Wildcat, but know this—I will always protect you, even if it's from yourself. Always." The heat of him suddenly disappears, leaving me cold and empty at the loss.

A sudden slamming of metal makes me jump. I whip my head to the side in time to see him walking around to my side of the car. Without a word, he opens my door and extends his hand to me. Blue eyes pierce through me, waiting, hoping. There's no sarcasm, no innuendo. Just Axel, baring a sliver of sincerity that lies underneath his surface. It's a small show of good faith on his part, and I despise how much I want to throw it back in his face, but I don't. I know when to let stuff go.

He pulls me to my feet as Zane emerges from the front office. Without a word, we follow Zane down a dimly lit hall. The entire way, I do my best to ignore the peeling blue paint and cracked matching stucco. It isn't until we make it up the stairs—since this fine establishment doesn't have an elevator—and into our room that I'm met with the real horror of our situation. All the effort Axel has just made becomes complete bullshit.

"Are you kidding me right now? One fucking bed!" I gesture between the bed and beige nightstands as I direct my wrath to the only one that can make my temper flare like this and do my best to ignore the musty smell of the tan carpet that looks like it's seen better days.

Axel shrugs and rubs his thumb along his bottom lip as his gaze stays plastered on the flower-covered wall over my shoulder.

"It's all they had," Zane growls from behind me, but my attention is focused on the bastard that's staring at the carpet like it grew a pair of legs. The one that won't make eye contact with me. The one that's giving away his one and only tell at the moment.

Rat bastards, the both of them. I'm about to kick said rat in his nuts when a door next to the tilted dresser catches my attention.

"Wait a minute. What's through that door?" My head darts from one pain-in-the-ass brunette to the other.

"My room, and yes, before you lose your shit again, there's only one bed in there too." Zane shoulders past me without another word. He barrels through the door and closes it behind him, leaving me all alone with the bane of my existence.

"You fucking planned this, the both of you." My finger bounces back and forth between him and the door to Zane's room.

"I'm good, but not that good, Wildcat." Axel's face lights up at the same time his lips spread into a smirk I know all too well. It's the same damn one that has had my own lips spreading much too easily for him. Ignoring me, he plops down in the middle of the bed like a damn kid and pats the space next to him. "Bed-time, Wildcat."

"I don't think so. I'll go crash with Zane instead. At least he doesn't talk much." My hands curl into fists as I plant them on my hips.

All humor leaves his face. "That's not happening."

"Wanna bet?" My feet only make it a step when his words stop me.

"You can try, but you won't even make it to the door before I catch you, and then I'm gonna tan your ass." A grin spreads across his lips as he pushes off the bed, not stopping until he's so far into my space that I can feel nothing but the heat of his breath against my cheek. The pupils of his blue eyes widen into a dark storm as we continue our stare-down. "Maybe that's what you want? Maybe you're remembering every dirty thing I did to you with these hands?" He holds up his hands and wiggles his fingers at me. Fingers that are rough and soft all at the same time. Fingers that caressed over every part of my body. Fingers that have been so deep inside me that I didn't know where he ended and I began.

I let out a deep exhale and do my best to bury the emotions that are aching to surface. I can't break. Not now.

Axel is like a big puppy—playful and sweet—luring you in and making your heart melt before he shits all over it.

I remind myself why puppies are really devils with tails and push past him to what he thinks will be my side of the bed. Without a word, I yank the comforter and a pillow off and go about making my own at the foot of the bed. It feels like I'm lying on a concrete slab, but I ignore the stale carpet and the way the material scratches along my skin and hunker down for a long-ass night.

Axel cranes his neck, watching my every move, and I half expect him to fight me on these newest sleeping arrangements. Instead, he grabs a chair from the nearby table and props it up underneath the handle. He must feel the heat of my glare digging into his back because he turns his head and winks.

Unbelievable. I open my mouth to tell him off, but then I remember this is Axel I'm dealing with. Pushing you beyond the brink of sanity is ingrained in his DNA, and I'm not taking the bait tonight. I lay back down and do my best to ignore him walking past me to the bed. The springs of the mattress squeak in protest as he plops down on it. I really hope one of them snaps and nails him in his delectable ass sometime during the night.

Our breathing echoes against the dust-covered walls as I wait for his to even out. I only have one chance at escape, which means I need to be smart about it. I feign sleep as best I can, plotting out how quietly I can move that chair.

"You can try it, but then I'll handcuff you to me until

we're back home. Night, Wildcat." I should have known better. Axel knows me almost better than I know myself.

My body tenses at the same time he clicks off the lamp.

Asshole!

7
KELSEY

Bang. Bang.

Each shot matches the pounding of my heart as we're covered in blackness. The tight grip around my arm loosens at the same time a warm wetness splatters against my skin. A couple of small thumps echo in the dark, causing me to jump.

There's a brief blanket of silence that hangs in the air, but once the lights flicker back on, it's nothing but complete chaos. A body is slumped over the table next to me. Blood pools out of the bullet-sized hole in his head.

I cover my mouth as my stomach rolls. Seeing a dead body in person is much different than it is on TV. More bullets fire through the air, and I need to get out of here before one of them lodges in me. My feet carry me out from behind the booth to the back of the club in search of the nearest door, but I don't make it very far when hands grab me from behind. "No!" My elbow jerks back, hitting a warm wall of muscle.

"Hmph." The hands around me loosen a fraction, but it's not enough for me to break free. I raise my arm ready to *strike again when a familiar voice whispers in my ear, "It's me, Wildcat. You're safe. Those fuckers can't hurt you anymore."*

My body goes lax in his arms as I'm finally able to breathe again. He's here. He came for me.

There's a scuffle behind us, and when I turn to face the stage, my blood runs cold. Another shot rings out, but this one has my body growing cold. Charlee's body falls to the floor as blood pours from her wound.

"NO!" I bolt upright against the headboard as the mattress creaks from the commotion. Sweat drips down my back as I shake off the images that are still trying to replay in my head.

"How long?" I jump at the sound of that deep voice.

"Damn it, Zane. You scared the shit out of me." My hand wipes away the beads of sweat dripping down the side of my face as I glare at the mammoth of a man sitting across from me. He's at least an inch taller than Axel and manages to make that table look like it's made for a small child.

"How long, Red?" His deep voice vibrates along my skin, causing my hackles to rise, and not in the same way his brother does.

I clear my throat a few times to stall, but I should have known better. Zane's will is a force to be reckoned with. He'll wait you out until you crack. Patience is his specialty. He kills you with it. When my throat becomes sore, I'm left with no other choice but to answer him. "How long what?"

"Don't play dumb. We both know you're much smarter than that." The sharpness in his tone has my head whipping up to meet his ice-blue eyes. It's been two years since I've seen him, but he looks pretty much the same. The only difference is that his beard is longer and he has a few more tattoos.

"After it happened, they came almost every night, but I got it under control. I haven't had one in over a year, but the other night..." My voice trails off, but I don't need to finish my thoughts.

"Triggered it," he finishes for me.

It takes everything I have not to squirm under his scrutiny, but I sit up taller and square my shoulders back as my eyes remain locked on his. I am not going to be intimidated by his attractive badass vibe, even if he has a great beard, amazing tattoos, and a killer man bun.

His dark eyebrows pinch together the longer he continues to watch me. "Did you ever talk to anyone about them?"

"Who would I tell?" A laugh escapes me, but it's as hollow and empty as I've felt for the last two years.

He runs a hand through the knotted mess of hair on top of his head before leaning forward and resting his elbows on the tops of his massive thighs. I swear I hear his black jeans stretch in protest under all that muscle. Muscles must be a familial trait. That and the ability to crawl under my skin like a rash.

I avert my eyes and let my gaze drift along his left arm, inspecting every single tattoo like it holds the answer to the universe. Most are beautiful, but there's one in particular that catches my eye. It's a black snake that crawls up his arm and peeks out from the collar of his shirt. He's too far away to make out much else except for the jade eyes that pop against the dark scales.

I'm about to ask him about it when he shifts in his

chair and draws my attention to a white paper bag dangling between his fingers. "Hungry?"

I nod, taking it for the peace offering it is. "Starved." The second I peel back the wrapper, I'm hit with the smell of bacon and sausage. I take a bite and do my best to suppress my smile as I chew, but it's hard because the mixture of salt and grease on my tongue reminds me of home. "I can't believe he remembered."

"It's Axel. He has the attention span of a gnat and the damn memory of an elephant." Zane shrugs.

I ignore the fluttering in my stomach at Axel's thoughtfulness and ask what I've been dying to do since they showed up. "How is she?"

The corner of his mouth curls into the closest thing I've ever seen resembling a smile in the short time I've known him. "Happy."

"That's good. Really good."

Zane pulls out his wallet and tosses a picture onto the bed in front of me. "Here."

Warmth spreads across my chest as I take in the dark-haired bundle in her arms. My finger traces over every detail. Charlee's green eyes have a light in them that I haven't ever seen on her as she smiles down at the baby in the photo.

"Her name's Lily."

Tears fill my eyes, but I wipe them away just as fast as they appear. "She's beautiful." I slide the photo toward him, but he pushes it back to me.

"You can keep that one. I've got plenty more."

"Thanks." I smile down at the picture and take another bite, but damn near choke on it when Axel strolls out of the bathroom, like the tornado he is, in nothing but a towel, whistling like a damn fool and destroying any semblance of peace I was enjoying. His eyes light up when he sees where I'm at and what I'm doing. "Morning, Sleeping Beauty."

"How did I end up in the bed?" I narrow my eyes at him, waiting for the answer I already know.

"Like I'd really let you sleep on the floor, Wildcat." He shakes his head and rummages through a plastic shopping bag that's on the dresser across from me while he continues to whistle.

"Put some fucking clothes on. I don't want to see your shit flopping around, man." Zane shakes his head and crosses his arms over his chest.

"Not my fault I got the bigger equipment in the family, Z." Axel ignores his brother and goes back to his task. At the same time, Zane shakes his head.

A flush creeps along my face as images of what Axel is packing underneath that towel flood my mind. I squeeze my thighs together to stop the aching that's building inside and force down the rest of my food.

"Hungry, Wildcat?" Axel laughs.

"It's no Waffle House, but I guess it'll do." I shrug and clean up the small mess of crumbs in my lap.

He raises an eyebrow at me. "Right." His phone vibrates against the wooden dresser, and his eyebrows pinch together when he reads who's calling. "Wildcat, go shower so we can hit the road. I have to take this."

"I don't have anything to shower with, genius." My hackles rise at his demanding tone. I'm not some little kid he can order around.

The corners of his mouth lift into a grin, drawing my eyes right to those damn dimples. I swear he does it on purpose. He tosses a couple of plastic shopping bags onto the bed next to me and makes his way over to the door with the phone and a cigarette in hand. "While you were out cold, in *our* bed, I went shopping."

I gloss over the bed comment and focus on the important part of that statement. "How do you even know what I like? Or what size, for that matter?"

He pauses, with his hand on the knob, and shoots me a look. One that has me ready to combust where I sit. One that's gotten me into serious trouble before. It doesn't help matters that he's still in nothing but that damn towel. "I remember everything about your body, Wildcat."

My mouth drops open as he shuts the door.

"He can't be serious!"

Zane holds his hands up in front of him and shakes his head. "Not getting involved."

I continue to stare at the door from the bed, at a loss for words. Between the food and the supplies, it's all too much. It's almost sweet.

Then he speaks and ruins it.

"Move that ass, Wildcat," he shouts through the door.

With a heavy sigh, I storm off into the bathroom with all my goodies in hand, but not before Zane has the last word.

"You have another nightmare, you tell Ax. Or I will."

I shut the door and lean back against it with my heart lodged in my throat. His words slice through me, opening old wounds.

Trust is a fragile thing, and once it's broken, it can be repaired, but it'll never be the same.

Wetness pools in my eyes, but I shake it off and clear

my head. Now, more than ever, I know what I need to do. And run I will. Because my heart won't survive Axel breaking it a second time.

8

AXEL

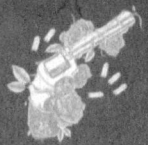

"Miss me, Hellcat?" I laugh and lean my side against the railing as my bare feet rub against the cool concrete.

"What part of *I want this shit handled quietly* didn't you understand?" asks a low, lethal voice that does not belong to Charlee.

"Ash?" My stomach drops at the same time my body tenses. I should have known he'd resort to using her phone when I wouldn't pick up for him. A cool breeze blows past, and I do my best not to shiver. Maybe I should have put some clothes on before coming out here, but the look on Kelsey's face when she saw me in nothing but this towel was worth every bit of hypothermia I suffered for it.

"Who the fuck else would it be?" Fatherhood has not mellowed him out one bit. He's still got a quick-trigger temper, well, unless it comes to Charlee and Lily. They get the teddy bear, and we get the beast.

"Oh, I don't know. Since it's Charlee's number,

maybe I expected to hear her sexy voice instead of having my ass chewed out by you, *Dad*."

"Cut the shit, Ax. You've been avoiding my calls for a couple of days, and if you do that again, I'm going to put my boot so far up your ass you'll taste the leather for weeks."

"That sounds pleasant." I hold the phone on my shoulder and light up a cigarette. Something tells me I'm gonna need an entire fucking pack when this conversation is over. "Did you just call to ream my ass, or does this bitch fest have an actual point?" I exhale a cloud of smoke and watch it float off until it disappears.

Asher grows quiet for a minute, and I brace for the volcano that's about to erupt, but to my surprise, he keeps his cool. "Both. I can't dig into this mess until I have more to go on. All I got from Zane was they were some Irish fucks who took shots at you. Who did you piss off this time?"

"Why do y'all assume that this shit is happening because of me?" My eyes narrow as I scan the cars in the parking lot, making sure our new friends haven't found us yet.

"Maybe because you've always thought with your dick and probably fucked over the wrong girl this time?"

An elderly couple happens to be heading my way, and I'm sure they can hear every word Asher spews from where they are. "Morning." I tip my head at them and smile like my mama taught me.

Their faces pinch together the closer they get. Both of their gazes trail from my towel up to the tattoos covering my chest while Asher is still in the middle of his rant. I take a long, slow drag off my cigarette and wink, causing their steps to falter for a split second.

A muscle tics in my jaw at Asher's bullshit, so I respond with the first thing that pops in my head. "You know I haven't gotten pussy in two years. I've jerked off so many times I'm surprised my hands don't have calluses."

The old woman scoffs, and her husband pulls her along faster until they're tucked away in their room and slamming the door.

"I don't have the patience to deal with your bullshit this morning." He sighs into the phone as crying echoes in the background.

"What's wrong with my wildflower?" Hearing her cry like that puts everything else on pause. Lily has us all wrapped around her tiny fingers.

"Nothing. She's just fussy and not sleeping much, which means between this and your shit, neither am I nor Charlee."

"Is that normal?" My eyebrows pinch together as I rub my thumb along my bottom lip.

"Fuck if I know. I just know we won't get any rest until you get your asses back here in one piece."

"Same, brother." I flick the ash from my cigarette over the railing and watch it fall, trying to soothe my itching need to have Wildcat at home, in my bed, where she belongs.

"Come straight here. Don't take Kelsey home, no matter how much she puts up a fight, until we know what's going on."

"Trust me, I'm not letting her out of my sight."

"Do you think she knows anything that might help us figure this shit out?"

"No. She seems to think this is all my fault. I'm thinking we need to have a chat with the governor. He's the one who hired us to come get her in the first place, and something isn't sitting right with me."

"Agreed. I've left a few messages, and he hasn't returned them." He breathes a heavy sigh into the phone, and it doesn't take a mind reader to know his gut is telling him something is up.

"You think he's ghosting us?" A muscle tics in my jaw at the thought.

"If past experience has taught me anything at all, it's that we can't rule out a damn thing until we have more information to go on. I'll keep digging, but you need to talk to her and see if she knows something about her dad or any of his business associates."

"I'll try, but I think I have better chances of getting punched in the balls."

He laughs into the phone. "She's going to make you work for it, as she should."

"Funny, fucker. It's your fault I'm in this mess to begin with." I shake my head and push off the railing.

"I told you not to keep playing with fire, but you didn't listen. Now, you've made your bed, and you have to lie in it. Suck it up, Ax. You've had pussy at your beck and call for years and finally have one that won't put up with your shit."

"This the advice you plan on giving Lily when she starts dating, because you suck at it."

"Goddamn it, Ax!" I hold the phone away from my ear to keep from going deaf as he continues to ream my ass. He sounds like a pitbull raging through the phone, and I probably shouldn't bust his balls like that, but what are baby brothers for? She won't be dating period, but it doesn't mean I can't have my fun. He shouts a few more times before hanging up.

I stay outside a few more minutes and finish my second cigarette until I feel I've given Kelsey enough time to shower and do all that girly shit she likes to do.

Images of her wet and naked in the shower have all the blood rushing south, but it's the fire behind her eyes when I piss her off that has my dick standing at full attention. I stroll back into the room wearing the biggest shit-eating grin and whistling the entire way.

9

KELSEY

I wipe the steam off the cracked mirror and stare back at my reflection. The water smelled like chlorine, but at least I'm clean after a couple of days of traveling. I don't look like I'm homeless any longer, so that's a plus. All the dirt and grime are washed away, but I have a few scrapes and bruises that have appeared since then. Purplish bruising contrasts against the green matching bra and thong set Axel bought me. I laugh at images of him shopping for my undergarments.

Zane and Axel's voices carry through the door, interrupting my thoughts, but I can't make out any of what they're saying. I slip on the skinny jeans and green tank top, which were another gift from Axel, as fast as I can and press my ear to the door.

"Not talking about this shit anymore, Ax." The front door slams so hard, causing the one I'm leaning against to rattle on its hinges.

I wait for a bit before I open the door and plant myself in front of the dresser. Keeping my eyes glued to the mirror in front of me, my fingers run through the clumps and get to work detangling the wet strands. This one is bigger and much easier to use because the broken one in the bathroom kept fogging over.

I'm so focused that I don't realize my mistake until Axel's reflection is directly in my line of sight. He's leaning against the wall with his arms crossed across his chest in a navy T-shirt that hugs all of his muscles in the right places and brings out the blue of his eyes. Black jeans mold to his legs like a second skin and give way to an equally dark pair of cowboy boots. Even fully clothed, the bastard manages to undo me.

I clear my throat a couple of times to clear away the images of him in nothing but the towel earlier or the way my mouth watered at the sight and ask, "Where's Zane going?"

"To check us out. The sooner we get back on the road, the better," he answers, but he seems like he's lost in his own head and a million miles away.

"Agreed." I nod and go back to attempting to tame the mess that is my hair. Axel managed to acquire everything I needed except for a brush, and trying to finger-comb curly hair is next to impossible to do without getting your fingers tangled in it.

My gaze can't help but drift in Axel's direction as I continue to battle with the knots. His eyes trail up every inch of me. It makes me feel naked—exposed to him, even though I'm fully dressed. I ignore him and continue running my fingers through my hair. He pushes off the wall, closing the distance between us until he's in my personal space. His hands grip the sides of my hips, and he pulls my back up against his firm chest, rubbing his nose along my temple.

"Ax..." The familiar scent of tobacco and cedarwood sends shivers through me as his hardness pokes against my ass. I fight against the onslaught of emotions that are threatening to pull me under because I can't afford to drown in all that is him again, but I'm losing that battle more and more the longer I'm around him.

"You smell good enough to eat." His teeth nibble on the lobe of my ear as his hands slip underneath my top and trace slow circles against the skin of my stomach.

"Please?" My knees shake from the softness of his lips brushing against the shell of my ear. The warmth of his fingers leaves a lingering swarm of butterflies in my stomach. I squeeze my eyes shut and revel in the sensations that are flooding my body. I'm so far gone I don't know if I'm begging him to stop or to keep going.

"I'll give you everything, Wildcat. All you have to do is ask." His tongue licks and sucks where his teeth just were. Heat spreads from my core to my chest, and just when I think his hands are going to move farther south and release the ache building inside me, he stops.

My eyes shoot open, and I'm about ready to beg him to finish when he asks, "How long are you going to be mad at me?" His chin brushes aside my wet hair and rests against my shoulder as his blue eyes meet mine through the mirror.

"I'm not mad, Ax. I'm angry and hurt. There's a difference." I swallow the lump forming in my throat and do my best not to shiver as he runs the tips of his fingers higher up along my stomach to the edge of my bra.

His forehead scrunches. "Why?"

"You used me and lied to me. Then I was kidnapped because of all the shit you were into, and I had no idea why. How am I supposed to believe that you're being truthful now?"

A second later, his hands fall out of my shirt, and he spins me around to face him. His hands land on my hips, holding me in place. "Listen to me and listen good. I never used you. Everything between us was real. Every touch. Every moment. It was all us, Wildcat." A muscle jumps in his cheek as he stares me down. His blue eyes burn into mine, branding me with every word.

My heart pounds in my throat the longer our gazes stay locked on one another. The tip of his thumb lifts and lingers across my bottom lip while the hand still around my waist tightens. His head leans down as he brushes his lips lightly across mine. The kiss is slow and hesitant at first, like he's trying to tell me something.

My hands fist into the soft material of his T-shirt, pulling him even closer, and our lips tangle into a bruising kiss. What started out slow and sweet has quickly morphed into something else.

"Y'all ready to go or what?" Zane walks through the door, bringing me back to my senses before I do something stupid, like let him in again.

I jump out of Axel's arms so fast I'm surprised I don't trip and adjust my clothes. Nothing like being caught to add cold water to my hormones.

Axel drops his hands and adjusts himself but doesn't move away otherwise, leaving no doubt that I just gave him a raging case of blue balls.

Zane's head bounces between the two of us, but if he has any idea what he interrupted, he doesn't say a word about it, and for that, I'm grateful. He watches us once more before spinning on his heels and walking back out the door. "I'll be in the truck."

It takes Axel a second to move, and then he has our bags in hand and is waiting for me by the door, but before we leave, I need to know something. "How did you know?"

"Know what?" His dark eyebrows pinch together.

"My clothes." I gesture down to my outfit.

A smile lights up his face, bringing out those damn dimples. "I told you earlier. I know everything about your body, Wildcat." He smacks my ass and walks out the door, leaving me wanting to both punch and kiss him all at the same time. One thing is for sure, the drive home will be interesting.

10

AXEL

I rest my arm against the top of the bench seat and let my fingers hang near her shoulder. She hasn't so much as spoken a word to me since our kiss, but I bet both my nuts that she's been unable to think of anything else since we started driving several hours ago.

My thumb traces along my bottom lip while my knee bounces against the leather as I shift to the side. Sitting still is not the easiest thing for me to do, let alone after touching her. It's been on replay in my head, too, but so has something else. Something that may undo whatever progress I made back at the motel this morning. I have to proceed with caution when it comes to her. One wrong move, and she'll scratch my eyes out, but I need more information if I'm going to find those ass fucks that torched Willie Mae and shot at my woman.

We've stopped for food and gas a few times, but otherwise, we've kept on driving. It's taking us a bit longer since we're sticking to side roads the rest of the way home in order to avoid being followed.

Zane's been eyeing me through the mirror the

whole way, waiting for me to ask Kelsey shit, but lucky enough for me, night has fallen, and I can't see his ugly face anymore. It also means time is running out because the first thing Asher's going to do is ride my ass about it when we get home.

A warm hand squeezing my knee pulls me out of my thoughts. "Can you stop doing that? You're shaking the whole damn seat, and I'm about to get carsick."

My body stills, and I force myself to relax. "Sorry."

She lets out a heavy sigh a few seconds later. "Out with it already."

"Out with what?" I widen my eyes and give her my best puppy stare. It's gotten me laid more times than I can count, but I should have known it wouldn't work on her. None of my usual shit does. She's different. And that's what makes her so fucking special.

"Cut the bullshit. You're rubbing your bottom lip with your thumb, and you only do that when you're nervous or lying about something." She arches an auburn eyebrow at me and holds my stare.

"Fine. I need to ask you something, Wildcat. Something personal, and you aren't gonna like it." I turn the interior light on and face her head-on. If we're doing this now, we're doing it in the light where I can see every reaction that flashes across her face and brace for what's about to come. It's like playing with a stick of dynamite, and I guess I've just lit the fucker up. We'll see how badly this explodes in my face.

She crosses her arms over her chest as she sits up taller in her seat. Every inch of her is screaming "fight or flight" mode, and I wish I had a better way to do this, but I'm pressed for time and shit out of luck. "What kind of questions?"

"About your dad." I pronounce each word slow and careful, like I'm talking to a wild tigress. And in a way, I kind of am.

"Okay." Her eyebrows pinch together as she waits for me to get to the point.

"Do you know any of his business associates or anyone who would want to use you to get to him?"

Her mouth opens and closes a few times, like a fish gasping for air. I brace for impact. And I get one, just not the one I was expecting. "Wow. You're even better than the last time. I can't believe I fell for your bullshit again!" Her tiny fist punches against the leather as she spins to face me head-on.

I jerk back against my seat as her words register and hold up a finger. "Hold the fuck on. You think what happened back in the motel was to get info out of you?"

"Wouldn't be the first time you've used me for information."

My jaw clenches as I press my fingers against the bridge of my nose and take in a few slow, deep breaths. If I don't, I'm going to end up leaving a handprint on her ass. "I'll tell you this one last time. Anything I do to you or with you is all me, Wildcat. The only game I'm playing this time is for keeps."

"Bullshit. I'm not falling for it again." A vein pulses on the side of her neck, matching my own throbbing heartbeat.

We're so locked in our argument that I miss Zane pulling off the freeway, something that's never happened to me before. The truck slows to a stop, and I pull away from her glare to take in our new surroundings. We're in a packed dirt parking lot of a bar that looks like it's seen better days and has several rows of Harley-Davidsons parked up front.

Kelsey's blue eyes widen, taking in our new surroundings as well. "Where are we?"

"Alabama." Zane runs his hand through the lump of hair on top of his head. One of these days, he's going to wake up and find that Asher shaved his fucking head.

"Where at in Alabama?"

"Fort Payne." His clipped answers are grating on her last nerve, but I sit back and enjoy the fact that he's the one in the line of fire this time and not me.

"Why are we stopping?" Kelsey asks, but Zane turns his head and shoots me a look through the rearview mirror that would have any other person pissing themselves, then shifts his attention to Kelsey.

"Because it's getting late, and I'm starving. Plus, it looks like you two could use a time-out." Without another word, he hops out of the truck and heads straight for the bar. The door slams, leaving us in strained silence.

Kelsey shakes her head and presses her hands tighter against her chest, drawing my eyes straight to her luscious tits that are straining to break free from her tank top. My throat goes dry, and my fingers itch with the need to feel the soft flesh fitting between my palms once again. The zipper of my jeans becomes increasingly tight the longer I stare. I cough into my hand as a distraction. Otherwise, I'm going to have her for my last meal of the day instead, and while I'm okay with that plan, she'd probably break my nose for even suggesting it.

She catches me staring and adjusts the thin fabric, but it doesn't do shit except give me a flash of her matching bra underneath. "It's a bit smaller than I normally wear."

"I know." My lips spread into a wide grin as I grab her by the hand and slide her out of the truck before she can ream my ass. The movement is so fast that she doesn't have time to argue until I have her standing upright on the gravel. If looks could kill, she'd have shot me dead several times already.

"This is a bar." Kelsey yanks her arm out of mine and wrinkles her nose at the sign above the dirty glass door. "You sure this is a good idea?" she asks as we walk up to the door where Zane's waiting.

"It's the only place open this late out here. You want to wait until morning to eat? I don't." He shrugs and walks inside, leaving us to follow behind him again.

Her head full of auburn curls whips my way, and the withering stare would make a lesser man shrink. It's a good thing I'm prepared to handle whatever she gives me.

"You heard him, Wildcat. We need to eat." I shrug.

"I'm not done being mad at you." She shakes her head and crosses her arms over her chest.

"That's fine. You can glare at me all you want while we feed you." I hold the door open and wait her out.

"Fine, but I'm getting dessert," she sighs as she walks through the door. My eyes go straight to her ass.

So am I, Wildcat. So am I.

11

KELSEY

Time seems to stand still as every pair of eyes inside the place turns in our direction the second we walk inside. "Sweet Home Alabama" by Lynyrd Skynyrd blares out of a jukebox that's something straight out of the '70s as a wall of smoke and the stench of stale beer punches me square in the face. From my place next to the door, I take in more of the room. If I thought the outside of this place was questionable, then the inside leaves no room for doubt.

Dust coats the wood-paneled walls that are covered with miscellaneous motorcycle memorabilia. Just behind the bar, through an archway, is a cluster of pool tables that are all occupied.

Axel interlaces his fingers with mine and pulls me out of my stupor to a small booth that's tucked away in the far corner of the room. The heel of my tan boots sticks to the concrete floor with each step, but I don't dare slow my pace until I'm seated in the booth between Axel and Zane.

"Hurry. I don't have all night." Zane grabs the menus from the napkin holder in the center of the table and passes one to each of us. I wonder if it would kill him to speak in more than short, clipped sentences.

We have roughly a few seconds to decide on what we want before a waitress comes over to take our orders. She writes it all down, takes our menus, and walks off to the kitchen to turn it in.

I rest my hands in my lap as I glance around the bar, ignoring the wall of heat coming from the body next to me. This place is definitely nothing like Gilley's.

Axel squeezes my upper thigh, bringing my attention to him. "You all right?"

"I'm fine. I just hope we aren't killed and buried in the backwoods tonight."

Axel tilts his head back and laughs. "Nothing is gonna happen to you. I promise you're safe with us, Wildcat."

"Right," I mumble and play with one of the many cracks in the table. His words do nothing to ease my nerves one bit.

After a few minutes, our food arrives, and we devour it in record time. I didn't realize how hungry I was until the smell of grits mixed with sweet tea fill the musty air. Nothing comes close to a good old-fashioned Southern breakfast. Full, I toss my napkin onto my empty plate and lean back against the ripped vinyl seat.

"Come on, Wildcat. Let's go play some pool." His blue eyes meet mine, and a flush spreads across my cheeks at thoughts of the last time we played each other.

Judging by the Cheshire grin on his face, his mind

has gone down the same path. He winks and glances in Zane's direction. "Coming, big brother?"

"Only to watch her kick your ass." Zane grabs his beer, slides to his feet, and follows behind us.

We walk to the first open table we find, which happens to be all the way in the back of the bar, with eyes on us the entire way there. At least no one has bothered us so far. They're just curious because we're outsiders, and I don't really blame them. Small towns are a very tight-knit group.

Axel grabs a couple of pool sticks while Zane sits nearby at one of the small round tables between us. Another group of guys that appear to be in their mid-twenties, like me, are playing at the table behind us. Kicking Axel's ass with an audience this time is going to be interesting.

He sticks a few coins into the slot, and the clanking of balls dropping fills the air. Axel hands me a cue stick and some chalk. Then he racks the balls on top of the green felt table, keeping one eye on me the entire time.

I chalk up the tip of my cue until it's coated in a sea of blue when an idea comes to me. "Care to make a wager on this game?"

"How much?" Axel cocks an eyebrow at my words.

"Not money." I shake my head and force my face to remain blank. "I win, you let me go back to California without a fight."

Axel leans his weight against the table as he works something out behind his eyes. "And if you lose?"

"Choice is yours." I tilt my head to the side and bat my eyelashes, luring him in.

"You sure you want to make that bet?" He rubs his

thumb along his bottom lip, causing my insides to dance.

Zane runs his fingers through his beard while watching our entire exchange in silence. His eyes meet mine with a hint of humor, leaving me wondering for a brief moment if I've just screwed myself. Then I think back to the last time I kicked Axel's ass, and my resolve strengthens.

"I am if you are." I square my shoulders and roll the wooden stick between my fingers, forcing the thrumming of my pulse to remain steady. This is Axel, and he can detect bullshit a mile away. I need to keep my cards close to my chest if I'm going to keep the upper hand with him.

Axel nods and takes the bait. He finishes racking the balls and backs away, holding his hands out for me. "Ladies first."

I manage to break and knock a couple of solid balls into two different pockets. On my next attempt, I scratch and bite my tongue. I will not be a sore loser.

The group of guys behind us are beginning to become rowdy the more they drink, but I focus on the game and kicking Axel's ass.

Axel makes the next several shots, and we continue to play back and forth until there's just the eight ball left.

"One ball left, Wildcat." He grins and takes a long, slow sip of his beer. The muscles of his thick neck moving in tandem with every swallow. My mouth waters at the sight as an ache throbs between my legs. Judging by the gleam in his eye, the bastard knows damn well what he's doing to me.

"Prepare to go down, Axel Savage." I wipe my sweaty

palms down my jeans and focus on the game. He is not going to get into my head. I'm going to hand him his balls on a silver platter and leave all of this shit in the past where it belongs.

The game's in the bag. I line up my shot, already mentally preparing a victory dance, when a cool wooden object pokes me right between my legs, causing me to miss and scrape against the felt. "Hey!" I spin on my heel to face the asshole that just touched me without my permission.

"Just playin' around, Sugar." The jerk with the mustache smacks my ass and walks off to where his friends are. I tense up, ready to beat him with my pool stick, when heat radiates from behind me.

"What the fuck?" Axel cuts in front of me and rushes up to the group. A heavy feeling settles in my stomach. Things are about to go from bad to worse. My head whips to the side in search of Zane, and the ass is still seated in his chair, sipping another beer like he's at a family picnic without a care in the world.

"Relax, man. We're just having some fun." Mustache Pervert laughs, and his friends join in like it's all some big joke.

"Fun is keeping your fucking hands to yourself and off my woman." Axel shoves him in the chest, knocking him back against the wall so hard a picture falls.

"Fuck off, asshole." He knocks Axel's hand off him and puffs out his chest.

Without warning, Axel's fist crashes into the guy's nose. Mustache Pervert drops to his knees and groans as blood gushes down his face.

"Son of a bitch! You broke my fucking nose." He cups his face, but blood spurts all over the place.

Axel hovers over him with his fist clenched. "You touch her without her permission, I do the same to you."

Mustache Pervert gets the message and stays down, but his buddies don't. One rushes Axel, but he's quicker and ducks the hit. The guy falls forward and ends up hitting a person at another table. From there, things spiral out of control fast. Everyone in the bar is out of their seats, punching the first person they can find. It's a sea of limbs and bodies flying everywhere.

Axel's got one of the guys from the original group by the throat when another sneaks up behind him. Before I can open my mouth, Zane is out of his chair and has the guy by the throat and pinned up against the wall.

"If anyone kicks my brother's ass, it's me." He throws a punch, but the guy breaks free, and the two of them start fighting on top of an empty pool table.

I bob and weave out of the way to avoid being hit but catch sight of one of the instigators creeping up behind an unsuspecting Axel. Oh, hell no! I grab a nearby beer bottle off the table and crack the guy over the head with it. He goes down, but then another one spins around, heading straight for me. I back up, preparing to grab another bottle, when Axel knocks him out with one punch.

"Time to go, Wildcat." He laces his fingers through mine and runs for the nearest exit, dodging as many flying fists on our way out as we can. Zane's heavy steps follow close behind, but I don't dare turn around, or else I'll slow us down.

We sprint around the corner, straight for Zane's truck. He uses his remote to unlock the doors, saving us a few seconds. My heart doesn't stop pounding from the time we jump inside to the time we're hauling ass out of the parking lot.

Zane doesn't slow down until the bar is a distant memory. The truck's cab is silent as the three of us do our best to gain control of our heavy breathing.

I slump against my seat, doing my best to get my heavy breathing under control, but it's damn near impossible. Then Axel's laughter breaks the silence.

"What's so funny?" My eyebrows pinch together as I wipe a bead of sweat off my forehead.

"You scratched. I won."

My spine stiffens. The hell he did!

12

AXEL

I'm so amped up after the shit went down in the bar that I'm wide awake the rest of the drive home. Kelsey does her best to fight sleep, but her adrenaline crash hits her hard, and she's out like a light before we even reach the state line.

We pull up the dirt drive, through the thick Georgia pines, and up to our two-story cabin next to Asher's silver pickup. It feels like it's been forever since I've seen those windows that align the front wall, separated by a stone fireplace and a wraparound front porch. Three wooden rocking chairs are lined along the front as well as a matching small table, but it's the one behind it that looks like an exact replica and the pile of baby toys in front of it that settles me down.

"You going to wake Sleeping Beauty?" Zane asks.

"In a minute." I hop out of the truck and stretch my legs. There's no stopping the smile that appears on my face the second I inhale the fresh Georgia air. It's good to be home. It's our own slice of heaven out in the woods and away from all the bullshit of the city. I walk around to her side of the car and take a minute to enjoy her sleeping form.

Reddish-brown lashes rest against her porcelain skin, and her red hair hangs in a curly mess around her face. There's not an ounce of makeup on her face, showing off the light dusting of freckles that cover her small nose, and her pouty lips are pursed. She looks like a kitten, all cuddly and shit, but I know once she's awake, the claws will come out in full force.

The muscles in my face twitch at the thought. I open the door and lean in until my lips are close enough to feel the softness of her cheeks. "Wake up, Wildcat. We're home."

It takes another few moments of coaxing before she finally stirs. Those blue eyes open. Warm and welcoming.

"Already?" She stretches her arms over her head, causing her tits to stick out in the process, making my mouth water at the sight.

I ache with the need to suck on her dusty pink nipples until they're hard and pinch them with my fingers. Great. Now, I'm hard. I shift to hide the bulge in my jeans and outstretch my hand to her.

"Come on." I avert my eyes before she can catch me staring and help her out of the cab into the fresh summer air that doesn't do dick to clear away the tension in my balls.

We walk to the front of the truck where Zane is standing and pause. He pulls out a pack of smokes from his pocket and offers me one. That should have been my first clue we were in for a world of shit, but I was too busy dreaming of soft tits in my mouth to pay attention to the signs.

As I'm lighting up, Asher storms out of his house like a wild boar about to be mounted. Nothing new there.

Kelsey tenses up next to me, looking like a scared kitten. I can only imagine what this must look like to her. Asher's a big fucker at six-two, and considering the majority of it is muscle, he would intimidate most people. If that didn't do the trick, then it would either be his tattoos or the fact that he still looks like he's fresh out of prison that might do it. Good thing I'm not most people.

"Hey, big brother." I pinch the cigarette between my lips at the same time I squeeze Kelsey's hand, pulling her deeper into my side.

His blue eyes bounce from me and back to Zane as his dark eyebrows pinch together. "What the fuck happened to you?"

"Axel happened." Zane wipes at the dried blood on his lip that I must have missed in all the excitement last night.

"It was not my fault." I whip my head back and forth between the two of them. They always gang up on me.

"It's never your fault." Asher shakes his head as he lights up a cigarette and stares me down.

"He grabbed my woman's ass. What would you have done?" I grind my teeth at the same time Kelsey gasps next to me, drawing our eyes to her.

A muscle tics in Asher's cheek as he blows out a cloud of smoke, letting my words sink in. He lets it go and gives Kelsey a quick once-over. If it were anyone else, it would piss me off, but this is Asher. He's hesitant to bring anyone new into the fold. Old habits die hard, and all that shit.

"That's what I thought." I rub it in deeper because I know damn well he'd do worse. Has done worse.

He opens his mouth, no doubt about to rip into me some more, when the sound of a baby crying shuts all of us up.

"You're back." Charlee bounces the dark-headed bundle in her arms as she comes near us. Her long dark hair is up in one of those messy knots that Zane likes to put his mop in. "Kels?" Her green eyes water against her olive skin the moment they land on the fiery redhead standing next to me.

"Hey." Kelsey's fingers tremble against my hand as she clears her throat a few times. Emotions war on her face, and I know this is hard for her, but it can also be the thing I need to convince her to stay.

Charlee hands Lily off to Asher before she wraps her arms around Kelsey so hard the two of them stumble back, breaking our joined hands. "It's really you."

"It is." Kelsey lets out a laugh that doesn't reach her eyes as she pulls at the end of her top. A small ounce of pride courses through me as the green color that I picked out looks hot as shit on her.

"We're going to go catch up. You got her?" Charlee asks as she grabs Kelsey's hand and pulls her along.

"I got her, Princess. You go on inside." Asher nods.

We watch the girls disappear into the house without a backward glance, leaving the three of us and one squirmy little dark-haired nugget outside.

Asher places Lily against his chest with one hand cupped around her little body and another cradling her head. Zane and I watch with blank faces while he settles her in place. He's so lost in his daughter that he forgets we're even standing there. Seconds tick by before he manages to pry his eyes off of her long enough to realize all eyes are on him.

"What?"

"Motherhood suits you." I cock an eyebrow at him.

His eyes narrow, and I'm sure if Lily weren't in his arms, I'd be sporting a black eye or two right now. He opens his mouth to probably ream my ass when he catches sight of Zane's truck. The corner of his mouth curls into a tight smile. "Where's Willie Mae?"

It takes only a second for his words to register. I whip my head to the side as my hands ball into fists. "You ratted me out like a little bitch, Z?"

"You weren't answering your phone." Zane shrugs and runs his fingers through his beard with a cigarette pinched between his fingers. I hope that shit catches fire. It'll serve him right. Neither one of them will ever understand the relationship between a man and his truck.

Asher presses a kiss to the top of Lily's head but never takes his eyes off mine. If he weren't holding my wildflower, I'd punch him in his smirking face.

"Fuck all y'all!" I storm into the house after the women. With all the bullshit that happened after that explosion, I haven't had time to dwell on the enormity of my loss. Now that Asher's shoved it back in my face, it's like sticking a knife in old wounds. I'll find the fuckers responsible, and they'll pay for what they did—to both my girls.

13
KELSEY

Charlee pulls me up a small set of wooden steps through the front porch and into the newer of the two cabins. "After riding with those two, I'm sure you could use some decent coffee and a bit of a break."

She leads me through an entryway that has an archway on my left that leads to an open living room with a set of double doors at the far end. A hollowness settles deep inside my stomach as I take in all of the baby stuff that's thrown around the room. It's proof that her life has gone on here without me. While I was stuck in my own personal hell, she was busy building a life. We're the same age but at entirely different places in our lives. I'm not allowed much time to dwell on it because Charlee nudges me further inside to the back of the house that opens up into a modern farmhouse-style kitchen.

She drops my hand and walks over to the sink where a fresh pot of coffee rests. "Have a seat," she says over her shoulder.

I take in every detail of the distressed wooden cabinets and marble countertops as I sit on the barstool at the island in the center of the kitchen. The corner of my mouth lifts into a small smile the more I study her decor. It's very artsy and all Charlee.

"Here you go." She hands me a bright red mug and leans back against the counter with her arms folded across her chest. Her features are much softer than when I left. Like a weight has been lifted off her shoulders, and with all the shady stuff her dad was into, it's no wonder.

"Thanks." The second the warm liquid hits my tongue, I'm in absolute bliss. It takes everything in me not to groan. Nothing compares to a homemade brew. My hands cup the sides of the mug as I keep my attention planted on the steam wafting off the dark liquid. A silence has stretched between us, but neither of us moves to break it. I shift in my seat and bite down on my bottom lip as the humming of the fridge fills the void. After a few more beats pass, I finally manage to find my tongue. "You look good. Happy." Motherhood definitely agrees with her.

"Thanks. I am. We didn't meet under the best of circumstances, but I think it all worked out in the end exactly how it was meant to be." Color stains her cheeks as she continues to talk. "Sometimes these things just have a way of working themselves out, you know?" Her words carry more weight than she'll ever know, and how I wish they were true.

I listen as she fills me in on the two years I've missed, and I absorb every word, fighting the tightness building in my chest.

"What about you?" She tilts her head of dark hair to the side, seeing more than I want her to.

I squirm, running through several scenarios. "Not much to tell here. I mainly just worked a lot."

"Still, it must have been nice living at the beach?"

"I guess it had its perks." I shrug and dip my head back down to the marble counter.

"I bet the views out there were amazing. I'd love to see your drawings."

The tip of my finger traces along the edge of my cup, enjoying the smooth, glossy finish as I fight the onslaught of tears. "I haven't picked up a paintbrush in a couple of years."

The front door slams, putting an end to our brief reunion. Heavy footsteps stomp along the wooden floors, and I know who it is without even turning around. Only one person can walk that loud. Then the door opens again, and two more—much quieter—sets follow behind.

Axel storms into the kitchen, nostrils flaring, but his demeanor softens the second his eyes land on me. The heat behind his gaze has my throat going dry. He plants a kiss on the top of my head before helping himself to my cup of coffee and taking the seat next to me. My body stiffens at this gesture. I'm still pissed at him, but I'm not going to ruin my time with Charlee by yelling at him in front of her.

Asher enters the kitchen, heading straight for Charlee. He wraps the arm not holding Lily around her and pulls her into his side, dropping a kiss to the side of her temple.

Zane is the last to come in. He doesn't utter a word

as he fixes himself a cup of coffee and hangs back near the fridge doing what he does best—watching.

With all three brothers occupying the same space, it's beginning to feel a bit cramped. Their massive forms command all the space in the room. There's no missing the family resemblance between them either.

Asher's gaze lands on me, and I fight the urge to squirm. The last and only time I talked to him, I was covered in Charlee's blood while we were fighting to save her life.

"Kelsey." He dips his chin in my direction. I return a polite nod of my own in greeting. His eyes stay fixated on me for a few more beats, causing my hands to clench tighter around my mug until I'm sure the ceramic might break. When I don't wither under his stare, he lifts an eyebrow and turns his focus onto the ass next to me. "We should talk."

"It can wait, Ash." Axel stands to his feet and stretches his arms over his head. The motion causes the edge of the T-shirt to ride up, giving me a slight glimpse of the wall of muscle he has underneath. Muscles that I've felt contract under my tongue as I trail down to my favorite part.

Heat builds in my core as the memories surface. My thighs clench together, and I bite back a moan that wants to escape. Then all of the lies he's told me surface. It's the bucket of ice water I need to return back to sanity.

"Ax." He lets that one word hang with hidden meaning.

"Let me handle it my way, big brother." Axel helps me up to my feet and ushers me toward the door.

"He's not..." Charlee starts from behind me, but Asher cuts her off.

"It'll be fine."

Axel never slows his steps until we're through the door of the other cabin and upstairs inside a bedroom. It all happens so fast that I don't have to process what's happening until I'm through the doorway, taking in the new space.

The walls are plain, but it's the oversized window at the foot of the queen-size bed that catches my attention. It takes up the whole wall, giving way to one hell of a view. Nothing but trees surround the setting sun for miles, reminding me just how secluded we are out here. Not good; I need to get out of here as fast as I can.

I spin around to face him and put my hands on my hips. "Where's your phone?"

"Why?" He lowers his head as he shoots me a look.

"Because I want to call my dad, and mine is thousands of miles away in my apartment." I straighten my shoulders, ready to force the issue if I have to, but he surprises me.

"Have at it, Wildcat." He slaps his phone in the palm of my hand.

My eyebrows crease. That was almost too easy. He's up to something. I'm not sure what he's playing at, but I'm not giving him the satisfaction of winning this game.

The phone rings until his voicemail picks up. I leave a message and hope to hell he calls back. The quicker he does, the sooner I can go home and leave this crazy asshole behind.

"No answer?" He cocks his head to the side, his eyes working something behind them as he takes his phone back and shoves it into his back pocket. He's a bit off, but then I have a light-bulb moment. Everything clicks into place for me.

"Nope, but you knew that he wouldn't pick up, didn't you?" My hands move from my hips to across my chest. "That's the only reason you even let me call him. What else do you know that you aren't telling me? Is there a reason he's not answering?"

"Nothing for you to worry about." His gaze travels around the room, landing everywhere but on mine.

"You're so full of shit." I shake my head at my own stupidity. Some things never change. I should have known better.

"Careful, Wildcat." He steps into my space until we're standing toe-to-toe. "I've been tolerant of your shit so far, but I'm reaching my limit, and you won't like what happens to you when I do." Heat pours off of him in waves, but I don't take it for the warning sign that it is because I'm seeing red myself.

"You don't scare me. I can't wait until I'm finally back home and rid of you for good."

"Right." His lips press into a tight line as he moves toward the door. "Sleep on it, and we'll talk in the morning."

"What are you doing?" I rush to the door, but I'm not fast enough to catch it in time before he closes it in my face. "You can't keep me in here, you son of a bitch!" I bang on the heavy wooden door with both of my fists.

The lock clicks into place, causing my heart to plummet into my stomach. My fists continue to pound against the damn, door hoping like hell he's just messing with me.

"I'll be back, Wildcat. Try not to get yourself into too much trouble while I'm gone."

Footsteps disappear, confirming the worst. I'm trapped. A damn prisoner in Axel's house.

How the hell did this happen?

14
AXEL

Blood pounds in my ears with every step I take down the stairs and into the kitchen. I light up a cigarette to calm my nerves before stealing a seat at the counter. Zane's leaning against the fridge with his arms crossed, tilting his head to the side and doing that assessing shit he always does—watching me for any sign of trouble. A cloud of smoke leaves me and billows in his direction.

"Problems?" He crosses his arms over his chest and tilts his head to the side. Those blue eyes never miss a fucking thing. For someone who's hiding demons of his own, he sure likes calling us out on our shit. And if I didn't understand the true weight of the burden he carries, I'd call him out on it.

"You could say that." I pinch the bridge of my nose between my fingers and fight off the migraine that's threatening to break. "I locked her up in Charlee's old room."

He cocks a dark eyebrow at me. "How'd that go over for you?"

"My balls are intact, so that's something." My thumb rubs along my bottom lip as a tightness twists in my chest. "She's so fucking stubborn. What else was I supposed to do?"

"I don't know. Talk to her?" He toys with the end of his beard as he waits me out.

"Tried that, smartass." I clench my teeth and let out a deep sigh. "She won't listen to a damn word I've been saying. I'm not letting her sneak out of here so she can end up headfirst in an even bigger clusterfuck than what we're in now. She'll see reason sooner or later. Let's just bank on it being sooner for my sake."

Zane doesn't say anything for once. He grabs some glasses from a nearby cabinet and pours us each a shot of whiskey. I toss it back and let the burn wash away the shit storm of the last few minutes. I'm just about to enjoy a small buzz when Asher walks into the kitchen and wastes no time with pleasantries.

"Ready to talk now, little brother?" He stands next to Zane and eyes the two of us for a minute. If he senses something, he doesn't say a word about it, which is fine by me. The less unsolicited advice I get from my brothers, the better.

"Yeah, let's get this over with." The tip of my thumb flicks the ash hanging off my cigarette into a nearby ashtray, and my muscles tense as images of Willie Mae up in flames flash through my head. My adrenaline spikes through me. Ordinarily, I'd fuck this out of my system, but since I'm sure that offer is off the table, I'd settle for a fight.

"Good." He slides a manila folder onto the counter in front of me. "I was able to hack into the cameras in front of her apartment building to make out a partial plate and a few of their faces."

I flip it open, shuffling through each image carefully. Some are grainy and hard to make out. Others are a bit better. My fingers flip through everyone until I come across a face so clear that there's no mistaking who I'm seeing. "That's him. That's one of the dickwads that shot at us." I stare down at the image, burning every detail into my memory for later. The bastard is going to regret ever pointing a gun at Kelsey when I'm through with him.

"It's not much, but at least we have something to go on. I'll run his image through a few different databases and see what else I can find. Things would be much simpler if Governor Loren would take my fucking calls, but it doesn't mean we can't get creative to find answers on our own." Asher rubs a hand over his dark, buzzed head.

"I had her call him and leave a message. Figure if he won't call you back, then maybe he'll answer for his daughter or at least return her call." I toss back another tumbler of whiskey and take another drag off my cigarette.

"Smart." He props his elbows against the marble counter and leans down.

"Don't look so surprised. I didn't just get the looks in the family, big brother." I tap the side of my head with my finger and go back to staring at the photo that's going to plague me until he's caught and taught a lesson.

Asher shakes his head but doesn't offer up a comment. He's mellowed a bit over the years, but not much. He'll still knock me on my ass if I push him too far. Too bad I just never remember where the boundaries are.

"What do we do in the meantime? Just sit here? Someone shot at us and blew up my truck. That shit isn't going to slide. I'm ready to show these fuckers how us good ol' boys handle things in the South." My hands ball into fists.

"We do what we always do, little brother." Asher's gaze hardens on mine. He feeds on this shit just as much as I do. "We go hunting."

"Fucking right, Ash. All for one and all that shit." My lips spread into a smile that I feel down to my toes. Redemption will be mine.

Asher takes the whiskey bottle out of Zane's hands to pour himself a double this time.

"You might want to go easy on that, or you ain't gonna be able to hear Wildflower if she wakes up tonight." I let out a small whistle. He hasn't drunk much at all since they had Lily, so this is surprising.

"It's Charlee's night." He shrugs and downs the drink in one go before slamming the glass down on the counter.

"In that case, we're gonna need a couple more bottles." I smack him in the shoulder as Zane pulls out two full bottles from our liquor cabinet, pouring us another shot. It's been so long since we've all sat and had a drink like this that I'm feeling all nostalgic and shit.

I raise my glass and eye each of my brothers. "To family."

"To family," Zane and Asher repeat at the same time before we tap our glasses together and toss the shots back.

It's late when we manage to polish off the rest of the whiskey. I'm slightly buzzed, but not drunk enough that I can't find my way into her room. She's curled up on her side facing away from me, looking like an angel, but the vision is too tempting not to enjoy up close.

I stumble further into the room, doing my best not to make a sound, and crawl in behind her, wrapping my body around hers. A groan rumbles out of my throat the second I do as her ass presses further against me, sending what little blood flow I have left in my head straight down to my dick.

We're a perfect fit. It's like she was made for me. Every inch of her is soft where I'm hard. Her porcelain skin is smooth beneath my touch as I trail my fingers up and down her arm. My nose brushes against her damp hair, and the familiar scent of mango fills my veins with warmth. She's like a cyclone—hot and dangerous all at the same time, but it's a danger I'd walk into happily. Whatever tomorrow brings, we'll weather this storm and come out the other side together.

15

KELSEY

I wake up with a furnace at my back. Warm hands are lightly stroking across the small expanse of skin where my shirt has ridden up. My stomach quivers with every touch of his fingers as they dip lower with each motion until they're grazing over the top of my panties.

Evidence of his arousal nestles firmly between my butt cheeks. Wearing nothing but a thong and tank top to bed may not have been the best idea. I was just so tired and angry last night after I showered that I fell into bed and passed out without a second thought.

"Morning." The warmth of his breath fans against the back of my head, causing another bout of shivers to race through me. His finger slides over my clit, and an aching fire of need explodes inside of me.

My body stiffens as my thighs clench together. It's damn near impossible to fight the urge to surrender to the sensations that are coursing through me. Only Axel has that effect on me, but then I remember how he locked me up in here last night, and all sense comes back to me. "What are you doing in here?"

"You know, generally, people follow that with a 'good morning.'" His body vibrates against mine as a laugh escapes him.

"Most people aren't locked inside a room all night like a damn prisoner," I shoot back while flashes of last night surface. Just like that, the spell I'm under is broken, and all I see is red.

His hands fall away, leaving an ache of emptiness behind. I hate myself for being so weak, so needy, when it comes to him. He falls to his back and lets out a heavy sigh, but I stay put on my side. If I can't see those blue eyes or those damn dimples, then I'll be able to remain strong and not be ruled by my stupid hormones.

We lay in silence for a few awkward beats, and I half expect him to say something else that will start another fight, but to my surprise, he lets it go and changes the subject. "You hungry? Charlee said she's making breakfast."

My heart warms at the thought of seeing her again. Yesterday, the short time we spent together wasn't nearly enough to make up for the years we were apart. "Yeah, I am."

The mattress dips as he gets to his feet, and my throat goes dry at the sight. Axel's in nothing but his boxers, dangling in front of me like a mouthwatering treat. That thin layer of material is all that was separating us from being skin to skin.

I shake my head clear of his six-pack and not be distracted by tattoos or the mouth-watering body they're attached to. "We should probably talk about things first."

He shakes his head as he throws on a pair of jeans and a navy T-shirt with some Southern-style writing on it. "I promise we'll talk about all this other shit between us later. Let's just go eat first."

"Fine." I scoot out after him and throw on my jeans, but when I go to put my bra on, my hands freeze. I have an audience. "Turn around." I motion with my finger for him to face the other way.

"Ain't nothing I haven't sucked or nibbled on before, Wildcat." His lips twist into a smile, putting my kryptonite on full display. Dimples that deep should be illegal.

"You are so annoying." I sigh and give him my back. After some creative bending and maneuvering, my bra's in place. Once I'm sure the girls are secure, I spin on my heel to face him.

He's still smiling like the cat that ate the canary, and I half expect him to gloat or make a sexual comment about my boobs, but once again, he surprises me by keeping quiet. Without a word, he grabs my hand and leads me down the stairs into the kitchen, where the rest of the family is. Let me just say the entire scene is a lot to take in first thing in the morning.

Asher's behind Charlee, whispering something into her ear that has her laughing, while his hands rest on her waist. Zane is sitting at the counter in a navy T-shirt and jeans, holding a very awake Lily. Her little hands are tugging at the end of his beard as he sips on his coffee without a care in the world. It's all very surreal.

"Sleep well?" Zane's blue eyes meet mine, and there's no missing the hidden meaning in his words that are directed at me.

"Yup." I force my feet to walk further into the room

straight for what I'm in dire need of, ignoring all the stares that follow along the way. Lucky for me, there's an entire pot of coffee that takes all my attention. I swipe one of the empty mugs next to the coffee maker and pour myself a full cup. The tips of my ears burn as I feel their continued stares, but I stay facing away from them to avoid eye contact. If I can't see them, then it's as if they aren't there.

Axel comes behind me, setting something down on the counter in front of me. My chest tightens the second I read the label, and my eyes flicker up to his. "Hazelnut creamer?"

"I told you. I remember everything, Wildcat." A smirk spreads across his face as he kisses me on the side of the head and steals a plate of food.

Not sure what to make of this whole thing, I move out of the kitchen and take a seat next to Zane. My gaze plants on Lily's wiggling form as I blow on the hot liquid in my hand, but I feel Axel standing next to me once again. This time I'm not succumbing to the bait. I keep my attention on the baby as if everything she's doing is the most fascinating thing in the world.

She's got her mother's green eyes, but there's no missing the Savage in her. Those same damn dimples that have been the cause of all my heartache and bad decisions. Decisions that have landed me in this latest predicament are on her chubby cheeks as well.

"Morning. Sleep well?" Charlee turns to glance over her shoulder at me with her spatula raised and Asher still snuggled up right against her. It's like they can't get enough of each other. It makes my heart melt. I love seeing my friend so happy. Her childhood wasn't the easiest growing up, given her dad's line of work, and she deserves all the joy she can find in life now.

"Morning." My eyes dart to Axel, and there's no missing the spark behind them as I answer Charlee. *The rat bastard!* "I did, thanks."

"Since the guys will be gone the rest of the day, what do you think of us having a girls' day?" Her green eyes light up as she speaks. "We can catch up like old times."

It's still early, so it takes me a second for the first half of her words to register, and then my head whips in Axel's direction, ready to commit murder. "Wait a minute. Where the fuck are you going?"

"No swearing in front of Lily," Axel whispers in my ear as he sets a plate of food down in front of him and digs in.

I pinch the bridge of my nose while I take a couple of deep breaths and count to ten to keep from murdering him in front of the baby. "Where in the *heck* are you going?"

His hand tightens against my hip, but he speaks to Charlee and ignores me. "I think that's a great idea, Hellcat."

My spine stiffens as my head whips in his direction. "Ax?" I press. He should know that an evasive answer isn't going to cut it. Not by a long shot.

A muscle in Axel's jaw jerks as he swallows. My throat goes dry watching the way the muscles in his throat flex with each movement. It's sexy. Everything the bastard does is. "Just out."

"Out where?" A vein throbs in the side of my neck. If he thinks his vague answers will appease me, he's dead wrong. I will find out what he's hiding. Out of the corner of my eye, I catch Zane handing Lily back to

Charlee, and then he and Asher leave out the front door to avoid being caught in the line of fire. They're definitely much smarter than their brother.

"I told you, I'm going to find those fuckers that shot at you." He shoves a spoonful of grits into his mouth as his eyes stay planted on mine.

"What does that mean exactly?" I ask as he shoves his plate of food in front of me. Damn him! He knows I can't resist a fresh plate of Southern grits.

"Exactly what you think it means." He kisses me on the top of the head and walks out of the house without another word, whistling.

I'm left sitting there with my mouth open. What the hell just happened? I turn my attention back to Charlee, and she shrugs like it's no big deal as Lily gnaws on her tiny fist.

"It'll be fine. You need to trust them. They know what they're doing."

Therein lies the problem, though, doesn't it? Because I don't. I don't trust Axel as far as I can throw him.

16

AXEL

I haul ass out the door before she can have time to question me further or follow behind. My brothers, the asshats, already snuck out, leaving me to face the firing squad all by myself. When Asher texted me of the plans late last night, I knew using a day with Charlee as a cover was the only way I could get away with leaving her here. I should feel bad about using Hellcat for this, but I don't. I've learned the only way to stay one step ahead of Kelsey is if I spring things on her last minute.

Minutes after we walk out the door, the three of us are buckled inside the cab of Asher's truck since it's the only one that isn't fucked up or blown to shit. I don't miss the pair of legs storming out the door in our direction. We're too fast for her, though, and her image disappears into a cloud of dust behind us.

"You do realize that your ass will be in the doghouse for that when we get back, right?" Asher keeps his eyes on the road as he speaks.

"Probably." There's no stopping the grin that flashes

across my face at the thought. "But I do enjoy taming the kitty."

"Damn it, Ax!" Zane shakes his head.

"Y'all brought it up. What did you expect? Just because you've been like a fucking monk the past few years, doesn't mean the rest of us have to go without."

"What's he talking about?" That draws Asher's attention, and he takes his eyes off the road long enough to glance in Zane's direction.

Zane's body tenses against the front seat, and I'm pretty sure if I were sitting up there with them, he'd have slapped me upside the head. I feel bad for outing his shit like this, but only for a split second. He needs that shove to deal with his demons, and the only one that can push him that far or even understand them is Asher.

"It's Axel. He's talking out of his ass like he always does." Zane plays it off, but there's no missing the glare he sends me from the window's reflection on his door. He's going to make me pay for this later.

"Right." Asher lets it go, but I know my big brother. This isn't over. He's just picking his moment to confront Zane, which means we're having another fun family meeting in the basement soon. And I'm not taking one for the team this time. They can beat the shit out of each other until he cracks.

Nobody speaks again for the rest of the drive as we head into an affluent suburb deep in the heart of Atlanta. I don't miss the way Asher's hands ball into fists around the steering wheel the closer we get. Not that I blame him. Charlee's father's old place isn't too far from here, and while we handled that situation, it doesn't mean we've stopped watching his men. As long as they leave us and ours alone, then we do the same for them.

Thanks to our business dealings with the governor, we're able to make it through the security gate and up the driveway without any issues. Things change the second we pull in, making my scalp prickle. There are no cars in the driveway. The lawn is overgrown, which is out of place since we know for a fact that the governor has a gardener attend to that shit twice a week. Something is off about this entire scene.

"Just like I thought. The motherfucker ghosted us." Asher slams his hand against the steering wheel as my temper flares. I don't like being used.

Zane hops out of the truck without saying a word. He knows when Asher's like this it's best to let him be, otherwise, you end up with a fist in your face.

"Well, while we're here, we might as well take a look around." I hop out and run up the stairs of the front porch with my brothers trailing behind me. An oversized glass door is the only thing standing between me and the answers I crave, so I do what any sane person would do. I reach into my back pocket and pull out my kit. The second I do, Asher sends me a strange look.

"What are you doing?" he asks.

"I'm picking the lock. Why? What's it look like I'm doing?" My eyes flick up to meet his stare, but my hands never stop working on the lock.

"Ax." His heated voice comes out as a warning, but I know I'm right and not backing down.

"You know another way to get in?" I cock an eyebrow at him because he's getting on my damn nerves right now.

"No." Asher shakes his head.

"At least make sure it's the right door this time." Zane shoots me a look, and I'm seconds away from pulling that damn bun off his head.

"Funny, asshole." I shake my head and go back to what I was doing. One fucking mistake, and they'll never let me live it down.

"He's probably got the place wired with alarms, Ax." Asher ignores us and keeps bitching at me. He's like a damn dog with a bone sometimes.

"Then you best be ready to disarm that shit fast." I twist my hands a couple more times before the lock finally gives way. "Let's see what big bad daddio's been up to."

Guns cock behind me as I put my shit away and pull mine from the holster on my side, mimicking their movement. I reach for the knob, but Asher puts his arm out, stopping me.

"Just know if the alarm company calls, you're dealing with that shit. Not me."

"Sure thing, Mom." I hold my breath as I push open the door because the last thing I want is for Asher to be right. My head cocks to the side, taking in every sound, but nothing greets us back. A deep sigh leaves me as I stand back and motion with my hand for them to go on ahead. "After you, ladies."

"Wise ass." Asher rolls his eyes but holds his gun out in front of him, stepping past me and further into the foyer. Zane and I pull up the rear behind him, doing the same thing, because who knows what kind of crazy shit awaits us. After all the shit we've been through, we're taking no chances.

Everything is lifeless and cold inside. The first thing that hits me is the stale air. This place has been closed up tight for a good long while. The back of my scalp tingles once again. Something is leaving a bad taste in my mouth.

"We'll check upstairs." Asher jerks his head to the side for Zane to follow him.

"You do that." I leave them to do their thing and go left through an archway, past the kitchen, into a hall that ends at a dark wooden door. I shove it open, and my earlier suspicions are confirmed. "Oh, shit."

Several things catch my attention the second I step inside. Shelves of books are overturned, a computer is smashed to pieces, and papers litter the floor. It's a disaster, but it's the empty safe that has that sinking feeling in my gut from earlier returning. Someone was definitely looking for something here.

I step further into the room, glass crunching under my boots the deeper I go, but it's the large-ass mahogany desk that draws me in. On top are pictures. Dozens and dozens of pictures. And they're of only one person—Kelsey.

My blood boils the longer I stare at them. They must have been watching her for a lot longer than we were. There are some that go as far back as the night she left me.

"Son of a bitch!" My teeth grind together so hard they crack. I stare down at those pictures as fire races up my spine.

"Ax, get up here now!" Asher's voice rings out through the empty house like a bomb.

It's the tone in his voice that has my blood racing from my chest to my feet. I haul ass out of the study and up the stairs. When I reach the room where my brothers are, Zane's kneeling on the ground next to Asher, but it's the dried pool of blood at his feet that has my insides turning to ash.

"Oh, fuck. Is that..."

"Yup. It's Mrs. Loren." Zane doesn't touch her, but both he and Asher take in everything about the scene that they can, filing the info away for later.

She put up one hell of a fight. Dried blood is caked in her red hair, which is the same shade as Kelsey's, and a few sprays of it coat her pale skin. The dark stains on her torn blouse and pants from knife wounds have me ready to punch a hole through the nearest wall. Whoever did this took their time with her. I don't miss the way Asher tenses up as he stares at the green Celtic butterfly tattoo that's on her right forearm. It's a simple design with small script written underneath it. I'm too far away to make out what it says, though.

"We need to get out of here right now." He pulls Zane to his feet and pushes us toward the stairs down to the front door.

We don't stop until we're inside the truck. Asher starts the engine and peels out of the driveway as fast as he can. We're blowing past the guard and on the back road, heading back to the house in a matter of seconds.

"You plan on sharing with the rest of us what it was you saw back there?" Zane asks after a few beats of silence tick by.

"It's nothing you need to worry about yet." Asher brushes off, but I'm not letting this go. Not when it involves Kelsey.

"My ass, it's not. Out with it, Ash." Secrets don't fly with me. There's too much at stake.

"It was her tattoo. Or more what was written next to it. The name Donnelly mean anything to you?"

"No." My eyebrows pull together, doing my damn-dest to figure out where the hell he's going with this.

"What about it?" Zane asks as he pulls out a pack of smokes and hands one to each of us.

"I've only seen it once before. Before I got out." He lights up with one hand as he shakes his head.

"She had a fucking prison tat on her?" That doesn't make any sense.

"Or she's related to someone in there." A muscle tics in his jaw, and I have a feeling there's more to this than her dad told me, and I will get it out of him later.

"This just keeps getting more fucked up. Every time I think we're getting closer to answers, we're thrown another fucking curveball." Out of nowhere, a jolt knocks me forward. So far, I almost hit my head on the back of Zane's seat and lost my cigarette in the process. "What the fuck was that?" I turn around in time to see a black Jeep ramming into us from behind. "Mother-fuckers are trying to run us off the road."

"Floor it, Ash." Zane smacks his hand on the top of the dash.

"Hold on." Asher slams his foot down on the gas, causing the engine to whine in protest from the force. The Jeep stays right on our ass the whole time. "You want to play, asshole? Let's play."

"We're not losing him." Today is one clusterfuck after another. I wrinkle my nose as plumes of smoke float up in front of me. "What's that smell?" Then my fucking balls start to burn. "Ow, shit! I'm on fire."

"Calm down. You're not on fire. It's just your fucking cigarette, you pussy." Zane rolls his window down and throws his own out the window.

I flick it off my lap and stomp it out as we're hit from

behind again. "Goddamn it! Teach these fuckers a lesson, Ash."

"Hang tight." Asher grips the wheel so tight his knuckles turn white.

"When I tell you to, turn the wheel to the left, Ash." Zane leans out the open window with his gun aimed at the Jeep.

"Got it." Asher nods, keeping his gaze on the road.

"Aim for the tires." I slap Zane on the shoulder as my eyes stay glued to the Jeep.

Zane nods but keeps one hand on the roof of the cab and the other trained in the direction of the Jeep, waiting for his opportunity to strike. They slam into us a few more times, but Zane holds his position. His training is coming in handy right now.

"Now, Ash!"

Asher does what he says. A split second after that, the right front tire on the Jeep goes flat. The movement is so sudden that the vehicle loses control and crashes headfirst into a nearby tree.

We pull up alongside it, ready to kick some ass, but we find two lifeless bodies on top of the hood.

Movement in the back seat catches my eye. "I got a live one." I lean into the Jeep and pull the dipshit out by his shirt. He's covered in blood and has cuts everywhere, but I give no shits. This asshole won't live much longer after I'm through with him, anyhow.

He groans and gasps for air like a dying pig as I slam him to the ground. Asher and Zane flank my sides with their guns out as we stand together as a unit, taking in the asshole who tried to kill us. When I get my first good look at him, I can't believe my luck.

"You've got to be fucking shitting me." I turn to Zane. "Look who caught up with us."

"Ain't that the dumb fuck from the bar?" Zane's eyebrows pull together when recognition hits.

"It is."

Asher folds his arms across his chest and stares our new catch down.

"No, please." The guy pleads like the whiny-ass pussy he is.

"The call is yours, Ax. What do you want to do with him?" Asher makes sure the guy knows he's my bitch, and it's up to me whether we play nice or not.

"Wait a minute," the guy pleads as blood drips from his dark hair and down his face, coating his mustache. "I can explain."

"Shut it." An idea forms in my head as his whimpers fuel the fire inside me, and my heart pounds with adrenaline. "Got any rope?"

Asher runs back to the bed of his truck and pulls out a decent length of rope. "This work?"

"That'll do just fine."

He tosses it to Zane, who comes to stand closer to me. He jerks the guy around by his wrists and hands me the rope.

"Make sure it's tight enough that he can't get loose." Zane doesn't look away from the guy as he speaks to me.

"Won't be a problem at all." I step forward and wind the rope around his wrists all the way down to his feet. When I'm through, he ends up looking like a stuffed pig. "Grab his other arm, Z. Ash, can you grab his feet? Fucker's heavy."

He screams the entire way to the truck, which is

annoying as shit. "You got something to shut his ass up?"

"Will this work?" Zane hands me a roll of duct tape from the bed of the truck.

"Perfect." I rip a piece off and slap it on the dumb-ass's face, mustache and all. "It really does fix everything."

"What now?" Asher asks.

"Now, we get him to talk." And maybe skin him alive.

17
KELSEY

It takes a few seconds of staring at the door to realize what the hell just happened. In the next moment, I'm out of my seat and storming toward the door after their truck. I'll be damned if I'm left behind like some damsel in distress.

Dirt and sticks stab my bare feet as I put my full weight behind each step, but none of the pain registers. I have one goal and one goal alone—get to the damn truck. Bastard must have known I would try that because their taillights are all I see by the time I make it down the front porch to where Asher's truck was parked.

"Asshole!" My voice echoes against the mound of trees that surround me. He may not be able to hear me, but it feels damn good to let it out nonetheless. Mid-meltdown, a black truck flashes out of the corner of my eye, and an idea forms. The truck still has damages from our road trip issues, but as long as it drives and can get me the hell out of here, I don't care.

I'll show him. When I lift the handle on the driver's

side door and find it unlocked, my heart thumps against my chest. I climb inside and start rummaging through the center console. If Zane's anything like his brother, his keys are in here somewhere. Nothing but receipts for fast-food places are inside. I slam the lid closed and tap my fingernails on the plastic. They're in here. I can feel it. My eyes skim along the dash up to the visor.

Is it really that easy?

I flip the visor down, and a pair of silver keys fall into the palm of my hand. "Thank you, Zane."

The second I stick the key and twist, all happy thoughts die a slow, painful death. Nothing happens. "No, no. Don't do this to me. Start, you piece of shit." My hands slap the steering wheel and I try it several more times, but the engine doesn't even crank.

I jump out of the truck, slamming the door, and throw my hands in the air. "Fucking Savage brothers!"

Everything in me knows they were behind this—all three of them, the rat bastards. I spin on my heel, stomping back into the house the entire way. The door slams behind me as I continue the rest of the way inside and into the kitchen, where Charlee's sitting with a cup of coffee in her hands, watching my every move.

"Everything all right?" She arches a dark eyebrow at me.

"No. I hate him. He's an overbearing asshole." I pace back and forth, waving my arms around like a crazy person. My mind is a jumbled mess of emotions right now.

She watches me for a beat and then sets her cup down. "I think we're going to need something stronger than coffee for this." She hops out of her chair and goes into the kitchen to pull out two wine glasses and a bottle of wine.

I freeze and pinch my eyebrows together as I watch her every move. "It's ten in the morning."

"It's four in Italy, and Lily just went down for her first nap of the day, which gives us at least four hours of girl time." Her green eyes light up as she waves a monitor with a red light at me and motions with her head for me to follow her into the living room. The excitement on her face makes it next to impossible to say no. And truth be told, I could really use some time with her.

"All right then." My lips twist into a smile as I trail behind her and take a seat on the nearest couch. "Fill her to the top."

"Yes, ma'am." She smiles and hands me a full glass. "Drink up, Kels."

An explosion of tart and sweet fills my mouth, and a moan escapes me. It's been so long since I've drank, let alone enjoyed it, that I down the whole damn thing in one go, relishing in the numbness flooding my veins. A few beats of silence stretch as I stare down at my empty glass and toy with the stem, stumbling for how to break it.

"How have you really been?" Charlee finally asks the question that's been hanging in the air between us like a lead weight since I arrived.

"I've been..." My voice falters as I struggle with how much to give away. "Lost."

"I'm sorry. I wish I could have been there for you." She puts a hand around my arm and gives it a light squeeze.

"That's just it. When I left, I just wanted to forget it

all. I wouldn't have let you in if I stayed. If anything, I would have pushed you away." Her shoulders droop, making me feel like an asshole for even thinking she wouldn't be the rock I needed to get through my shit. I move on and change the subject to something else, something much less hurtful. "How have you coped so well with everything?"

She sags deeper into the couch and sighs. "I was a lot like you. Pissed as hell at first, but I don't know. Losing my dad kind of put things into perspective. Nobody's perfect. We're all flawed in some way, and that's what makes us who we are. I mean, don't get me wrong. I wanted to flay Asher alive at first, but then things changed between us. He wasn't just the asshole who kidnapped me but a man who lost everything at the hands of my father's men. I can't say I wouldn't do the same thing if I was in his shoes. Eventually, we fell in love, and it makes you do crazy things." She takes a big gulp of her wine as her eyes zone out.

"Like have a Savage baby?" I nudge her shoulder and smile because, at the end of the day, I couldn't be happier for her.

Charlee laughs. "Exactly."

"You two getting married any time soon?" I lean in closer to her and pour myself another glass of wine.

All laughter leaves her face, and her lips twist to the side. "I'm not sure."

"Does that bother you?"

She shakes her head. "I don't think Asher's ready. He's moved on with what happened to his first wife, but in a way, he hasn't. That's the last piece of Lauren he has left, and it doesn't feel right to take that from them. You know?"

"I do, but at the same time, it isn't fair to either one of you to let the past dictate your future. She was murdered, but that doesn't mean anything like that will happen to you."

"More wine." She changes the subject, and that's fine. I'm sure I struck a nerve and reopened old wounds.

We spend the rest of the afternoon catching up, and it's like time hasn't passed at all between us. We're the same crazy college kids, groaning our way through life.

"They've been gone for a while." I glance out the window at the cloudy sky. Looks like we are in for one hell of a storm later. "You sure we shouldn't call the police?"

"I'm sure they're fine." She waves my words off with her hand and sips more of her wine. After Lily woke up from her nap, we ate and sobered up somewhat. Once she went back down for another nap, we picked right back up where we left off.

"I guess you're right." Tears pool in my eyes as I stare down at my empty glass. I blame the alcohol for my sudden onslaught of emotions as images of Axel flood my head. "I hate that the lying bastard still makes me feel things."

"Oh boy. We're going to need the big guns for this. Hold on, chica." Charlee runs into the kitchen, messes around, and then runs back out with two tumblers and a brand-new bottle of whiskey.

"Is that from Asher's stash?" The corners of my eyes crease as I wipe at the stray tears that have fallen down my cheeks.

"Nope." Her green eyes brighten as she bounces on her feet. "This one's Axel's."

"Give it here." I motion with my hand for the bottle. "Looks like we're getting fucked up then."

"Yes, we are." She clanks her glass against mine and we toss our drinks back in one go.

"Holy shit! That burns." A cough escapes me as a fire races up my throat and spreads across my face.

"It does." Charlee nods but pours us each another drink. We down the shot, and then Charlee perks up. "Good thing it's Asher's turn to get up with Lily tonight because Mama is not going to be able to do it."

We laugh and devour more of the bottle as we get lost in simple conversation. This is what I've been missing for the past two years. I've made acquaintances, but I kept them at a distance. None of them ever saw the real me. Not like Charlee, she's the only one who ever saw the real me.

Out of the blue, Charlee jumps up to her feet. "Oh, follow me! I want to show you something." She pulls me up from the couch and onto my feet so fast that I have to brace against the arm of the couch to keep from falling over.

We stumble down the hall and into one of the back rooms that have remained hidden since I first arrived. Now that I've had time to explore more of this house, I'm realizing that it's much bigger than I first thought. Looks are very deceiving, like Axel himself.

"Wow!" My jaw drops as I take in every single detail.

An easel is set up facing the only window in the room as rain starts to pound against the glass, and the view is something you'd see in a magazine. It's every artist's dream studio. An entire blank canvas waiting for a unique spark of color to breathe life into it.

Charlee watches me take it all in for a few seconds before she asks, "You still paint?"

"No. Not since I left." A lump forms in my throat at another thing that I was stripped of that night, but then an image of a freaking cat hidden in the corner of the far wall catches my attention, and my heart sputters.

"Maybe you just haven't had the right inspiration." Her face lights up as Lily's cries echo through the monitor. Motherhood has made her too damn intuitive for her own good.

Then a truck door shutting breaks through my thoughts. My insides tremble, and my fingers hum with anticipation. Time to deal with my Savage.

18

AXEL

All three of us keep to ourselves the entire way out to the farm, which is fine by me. I need a minute to collect my thoughts and figure out what's going on. The last time we were here was at night, but everything looks the same. Pigs squeal off in the distance as Asher pulls up to the barn and puts the truck into park.

` I'm out and at the bed of the truck before he can even take the key out. My fingers are itching to get to the bottom of this shit. I open the tailgate and flash our catch a smirk. "Enjoy the ride?"

He shouts something, but it's muffled behind the duct tape.

Zane meets me at the bed and helps me to drag the guy to the edge of the tailgate. Asher stands on my other side and joins us because hauling this guy around is a three-person job.

"Where we taking him, Ax?" Asher asks as he secures the rope binding the guy's legs in his hands.

My eyes dart around the property when they land

on the red barn. An idea forms, and today just got a lot more interesting. "To the barn." He'll squeal like a stuck pig when we're through with him.

The sack of shit struggles as we carry him through the door and over to the far corner of the barn. We set him down on his knees under one of the giant hooks that are hanging down from the ceiling.

"We can't string him up if he's hog-tied." Zane scratches the side of his beard.

"Just a sec." I bend down to take a knife out of my boot before I slice through the rope freeing his feet. As soon as he's loose, he drops to his side and kicks his legs out like a wild boar. We jump out of the way in time to avoid being hit, but he takes advantage and rolls away toward the door. Too bad for him, we're quicker.

Zane stops him with his boot and stares down at him like he's a fly on shit. "Where you going?"

Asher grabs him under his arms while Zane takes up the other side, and together they drag him back to me.

"All right, let's hang up this fresh slab of pork." I slap his shoulder and laugh when he trembles under my hands. He should be afraid.

I take his hands and push the hook through the rope until he's strung up with his feet dangling above the ground. Asher and Zane step back once he's secure, letting me run the show.

I'd prefer to take my time and use something more creative to torture my answers out of him, but after what we found back at the house, the quicker I can get back to Kelsey, the better.

My fist slams into the side of his head, causing his teeth to knock together. Droplets of blood splatter on my face and onto my T-shirt, but it doesn't stop me. Feeling his bones crunch underneath my hands is one hell of a rush, one that I plan on riding to the very end. I let all my pent-up emotions out on the bastard. Over and over my fists connect with his flesh. My breathing becomes heavy, but I burn with the need for more. the need to make him bleed.

"Ax!" Asher shouts, causing me to pause mid-swing. "We can't ask him shit if his jaw's broken."

"Whoops. I guess you're right." I drop my hand and grab a fistful of his blood-caked hair, forcing him to look me in the eye. My finger grips the side of the tape and rips it off in one go, taking a good amount of mustache with it. He yells, but it falls on deaf ears. "Care to explain what the fuck is going on? Or do I need to persuade you some more?"

"Finn's going to have your fucking balls for this." He spits out a mouthful of blood onto my face.

"Finnegan Donnelly?" Asher tilts his head to the side, something working behind his eyes. I'll ask him what that's about later.

Instead of answering, the idiot smiles showing nothing but a mouth full of bloodstained teeth.

"Answer my brother, dickhead." I send a solid hit to his gut, causing him to choke for air. If he were standing, he'd be curled in a ball on the floor by now. I wait, but he still doesn't give, so I deliver a couple more blows. One to the ribs and another one to his side that has him groaning like a little bitch. Kidney shots are always the worst.

Zane and Asher watch me work in silence with cigarettes hanging from their mouths like we're at a ball game, and I guess to our family, this is a sport.

"All right! I'll talk." He gasps for air and hangs his head.

"Now we're getting somewhere. See how easy that was?" I wipe my bloody knuckles on my jeans and wait for him to spill his guts.

"Donnelly just wants the girl."

"I'm afraid we're going to need more info than that to stop us from cutting off your nuts and feeding them to you."

"We heard what went down in California, so he had us following after you for her own protection. Her dad is in over his head and owes debts he can't pay. We tried to save her mom, but we were too late."

"Bullshit." My fists curl at the images his words cause. I'm going to have to tell Kelsey about her mom, and that has a knife digging into my chest. She's going to blame that on me too.

"I'm telling you the truth. I swear it. Y'all have to believe me."

"We ain't got to do shit," Zane spits, never taking his eyes off him.

I grab a blowtorch off of the nearby workbench and toss it up in the air a few times. His blue eyes never leave it, but there's no missing the rapid rise and fall of his chest. "You know I still owe you for touching her without her permission."

"It was an accident." His eyebrows pinch together, fueling my rage.

"You're a real piece of shit! I guess we're going to have to roast your nuts and feed them to you after all." I flick the switch with my thumb and stare at the blue flame, while I say to my brothers, "Get his pants."

Zane and Asher move to do that when he squeals. "Wait! There's more."

My head cocks to the side as I stare him down. I let his heavy breathing fill the musty barn air and stare him down in silence. The longer I take, the longer the humidity gets to him, and that's enough to make anyone go insane. Georgia summers are brutal for that reason alone. Beads of sweat pool along the side of his head, and I know we're getting closer to the breaking point. Time to kick things up a notch because he's getting on my last nerve. "Start talking and don't stop until you've explained it all. Otherwise, it'll be your nuts roasting over an open fire, got it?"

"Yeah, I got it. Her dad fucked over the wrong people and racked up a debt he can't pay off. The people he owes want their money, and the bastards don't care how they get it. Since they can't find him, she's the next best thing. They plan to use her up and then sell her to the highest bidder when they're through."

A knot forms in my throat the more he talks. I knew something was wrong when the governor skipped town and we found his wife murdered, but I didn't think things were this fucked up. A vein throbs on the side of my neck as flashes of what they have planned for my woman flood my mind.

"Over my dead fucking body will they ever fucking touch a hair on her head. She's mine, and we won't let those sons of bitches near her." A tightness builds in my chest. They touch her, and there will be hell to pay.

"Christ, you're thick-headed. Have you listened to a fucking word I said?" He spits a mouthful of blood onto the ground near my feet.

"What's that?" I flick the flame back on and chuckle as he snaps his mouth shut. "That's what I thought."

He swallows and waits until I turn off the blowtorch to decide it's safe to talk again. "The three of you can't take them on all on your own. They have connections in high places. You need Finn's help if you want to keep her safe." His brown eyes darken as he stares me down. Dickhead has balls. I'll give him that.

I toss the blowtorch over my shoulder and pace slowly in front of him. Parts of his story are true, and I have a feeling the other half is only a partial truth. "Explain something to me. Why do any of you care so much about what happens to her?"

"We're merely concerned about keeping the order of things. They get messy if you fuck with someone as high profile as the governor's daughter, and it's bad for business." His body tenses as he looks everywhere but at me. Bastard is still hiding something.

I stop in my tracks and point the tip of the blowtorch at him. "I wasn't born yesterday. You're lying. There's more to it than that."

He shrugs. It's obvious he's not going to give me much more, and I'm tired of listening to him, so I rear the fist of my free hand back and knock him out.

"What now?" Asher asks.

"Now we go home and do some digging on this Donnelly douche."

"What about him?" Zane jerks his beard in the direction of the limp body hanging from the rafters.

"Take him down and tie him up next to the horse trough for now. I want to make sure everything he said is true before we gut him." I shrug and walk out to the truck, leaving Asher and Zane to handle him. I do it, and I might end up setting him on fire for the hell of it. Plus, I'm ready to get the fuck out of here.

Asher and Zane stroll out of the barn and climb inside the truck after a few minutes, but neither of them attempts to speak to me. They know I have a lot of shit floating around in my head and am in no mood to talk.

We pull onto the highway, and a dull ache in my fingers spreads to my hands. My adrenaline is wearing off, making me feel the full effect of what I did, but I'd do it all over again in a heartbeat.

A couple of miles pass us by before Asher clears his throat and I glance up to meet his eyes through the rearview mirror. "It'll be all right, Ax. She's safe at home with Charlee. You know we have your back on this, little brother."

"I do. I just hope she's still there." I wouldn't put it past her to hotwire Zane's truck. It has some damage, but I know that wouldn't deter her one fucking bit.

As if reading my thoughts, Zane twists in his seat and pulls out a black cube with four prongs on it toward me. "Kind of hard to go anywhere without this."

"You took your relay out? Good thinking, brother." I slap him on the shoulder and lean back in my seat. That's one thing off my chest, for now. It's a good thing Charlee's SUV is hidden in the garage out back and that she knows not to leave anywhere alone when things are like this. Otherwise, Kelsey would be long gone by now. Not that I don't enjoy the chase, but we don't have time for a game of cat and mouse at the moment. I need a clear head to plan our next move. When I do, they'll be sorry they ever fucked with a Savage. And whether Kelsey likes it or not, a Savage is what she is now.

19

KELSEY

"Wildcat!" Axel's steps echo through the house, causing my heart rate to spike the closer they get.

All thoughts of the art room vanish as Charlee and I stumble out of the back of the house and make our way to the front. My balance is complete crap right now. We definitely drank a bit more than I thought. When we make it into the kitchen, we find all three of the Savage boys' massive forms taking over the entire space. They're drenched. Droplets of water drip off their clenched jaws as all of their gazes land on us. Something has them on edge, and that thought sends a tingle up my spine.

"I'm right here." My hip presses against the counter to keep myself from swaying side to side.

He moves forward so fast that even if I weren't battling the effects of the whiskey, I wouldn't be prepared for it. One moment, he's standing there, brooding at me, and the next, his hands are gripping the sides of my face while his lips devour mine. It's a bruising kiss. One that's meant to dominate, meant to own me from the inside out—and it does.

All tension leaves his body when he pulls back. His eyes meet mine with an intensity that I feel down to my toes. "They ain't gonna touch you." His thumbs continue to stroke small circles against my cheeks, but it's the thickening of his accent that has me on edge.

"What are you talking about? What happened?" My hands interlace with his as I shake my head clear and take in the full effect of his appearance. His clothes have dark red splotches all over them, as do his cheeks, but the cuts on his knuckles are what make my pulse quicken.

"Is that blood? Are you hurt?" I break our connection and let my eyes roam over his body, inspecting him from head to toe for any sign of injuries.

"It's not mine."

"What have you done, Axel?" A lump forms in my throat as his words ricochet inside my head.

"Exactly what I told you I'd do—keep you safe." His fingers dig into the side of my face as he brings me back in and kisses me again. This time, the kiss is different. It's much slower, like he's taking the time to savor every inch of my mouth. His lips dance across mine a few more times before he breaks away and rests his forehead against mine. "You been hitting the whiskey, Wildcat?"

"Some." I lick my lips and let the taste of us linger in my mouth while I do my best not to fall over.

"How much have you had to drink?"

"Not nearly enough." I can't think when he's this close to me. The smell of cedarwood and tobacco clogs my senses.

"Wildcat, I asked you a question, and it's important that you answer honestly." The fingers wrapped around the side of my head stroke against my cheek in small circles. "How much have you had to drink?"

"I don't know. We had wine, and then we got bored and switched to your whiskey."

"We, Princess?" Asher breaks us out of our bubble, and we separate just enough for Axel to wrap his arm around my shoulder.

Charlee's cheeks heat as she braces against the counter for balance. She holds up her hand and pinches her fingers together to show Asher how much, but her lack of coordination now causes her to sway. "Just a little bit."

"Y'all are shit-faced." Leave it to Zane to be a buzzkill.

"Are not," Charlee and I shout back. It feels like we're a couple of toddlers he's just scolded.

"Where's Lily?" Asher cocks his head to the side, ignoring our outburst, as his eyes work something out. Whatever it is, it causes the blue of his irises to deepen.

"Upstairs sleeping." Her dark eyebrows pinch together as she answers him.

"Let's go, Princess." Asher grabs Charlee by the arm and takes the baby monitor from her hands as he begins to usher her out the front door, but she jerks against him.

"What about Lily?" she asks.

Asher's steps never falter as he shoves the monitor into Zane's stomach and shoots both him and Axel a look over his shoulder, doing that weird silent communication thing these brothers do. "Z's got her."

Zane doesn't say a word as he cradles the monitor in

his hand and disappears into the living room without a backward glance.

Axel takes advantage of that distraction and spins me around in the direction of the stairs. "Come on, Wildcat."

"Where are we going?" I hold on to the railing to keep from face-planting. Falling while going upstairs won't help my cause any.

"To your room. We need to talk."

My stomach twists into a knot at his words. "Can't we do that out here?"

"No." His features soften for a split second before he continues walking with me in tow.

When we reach the room he locked me in earlier, I tense up, but he squeezes my fingers as he leads me inside. His hold drops as soon as we enter the room. He shuts the door behind him, leans his back against it, and rubs the tip of his thumb along his bottom lip as his blue eyes stay fixed on me.

I do my best to tamp down the emotions that are threatening to swallow me whole and hold my head high. Silence stretches between us, but he never breaks it. The longer he stares, the more my heart pounds against my chest. My stomach rolls as I swallow down the lump forming in my throat.

"What is it? Just tell me!" My voice comes out louder than I intend, but it can't be helped. Whatever he has to say is going to gut me. I know it.

"I went by your house today to see what's going on with your parents and why they aren't returning our calls." He leans against the door and rubs his thumb along his bottom lip.

I want to scream at him for going without me, but

something about his body language tells me there's more to it. "And?"

He opens his mouth to speak but pauses for a second, collecting his thoughts. "We found your mom."

"That's good." I sag down against the mattress, nodding my head. Hearing his words is like a weight has lifted. I don't know whether to hug him or smack him for scaring me like that.

"No, Wildcat. We *found* her. Found her body." Every muscle in his body tightens the longer his gaze holds mine. "She was stabbed."

It takes a few seconds for what he's really saying to penetrate, and when it finally does, the floor falls out from under me.

"No! You're lying." Tears fall down my face as everything he's saying manages to sink in and sober my ass right up. Numbness takes over. It feels like I'm floating out of my skin. This can't be happening. "She's not dead. She can't be." My vision narrows as a tightness crushes my chest, causing my lungs to struggle for air.

Axel crosses the room in a couple of strides and kneels down at my feet. His fingers interlace with mine as a muscle in his jaw jerks. "I'm so sorry, Kelsey."

I sag against him and let all the pain out. He gets to his feet, pulling me into his arms, and he lays us back against the mattress. The wetness from his clothes seeps into mine as he holds me tighter, but it doesn't penetrate through my numbness.

"Is that her..." I can't even bring myself to finish that thought as I take in the red splatters on his face once again.

He shakes his head. "It's someone else's blood."

Neither of us speaks as his head dips against mine,

but words aren't necessary at the moment. All that matters is what he's offering me. We lie chest to chest, listening to the rain pound against the roof as his hands lightly caress my back. Every stroke pulls me deeper into his web, and it isn't long before my body craves more of his comfort.

"Let me hold you tonight, please?" His arms squeeze me tighter against him, and I don't fight him. I need this connection. This familiarity. Despite everything, his arms are the only place that I have ever truly felt safe. Felt like home. It's been two years, and that fire is still there, burning bright between us. I curl deeper into him and let the tears fall until I'm all cried out.

Every limb on my body feels like jelly, and my eyes become so heavy that I can't keep them open. I let the emotional trauma from the day pull me under. My heart's still in tatters on the floor, but I'll pick up the pieces tomorrow and do what I do best—survive.

20

AXEL

The sun beats down on my face, but it's the warm body next to me that has my dick springing to attention. As much as I'd love to wake her up and bury myself deep inside her, I know now is not the time. She needs her sleep. Last night was an emotional mindfuck for her, no doubt. Against the protest of my dick, I slide out of bed and throw on some gray sweats that I stashed in here earlier yesterday and do one last glance at her. Her eyes are red and puffy from crying, but she's still as beautiful as ever. I drop a kiss on top of her head and head downstairs.

The house is quiet, but there's music coming from the basement. A smile cracks on my face. Of course, their asses would be up this early, beating the shit out of each other. A Savage brother knows only one of two ways to release our stress—fighting or fucking. After last night, I'm assuming Asher's indulging Zane.

When I enter the homemade gym, Zane and Asher are on the mats in a boxer stance with "Du Hast" by

Motionless in White blaring through the system's speakers. Both have fresh cuts on their faces and lips, so they must have been going at this for a while.

"Started without me, did ya?" I steal a cigarette from a pack lying on the nearby table and light up as I watch them kick the shit out of each other.

They both shoot me a blank look and then go back to it. Asher bobs and weaves, avoiding Zane's fists. It's all very smooth. Very choreographed. The need to shake things up a bit hits me—hard.

"Hellcat not wear you out enough last night?" I shouldn't push Asher this early in the morning, but what kind of little brother would I be if I didn't take advantage of a golden opportunity to get under my brother's skin when I could?

Asher freezes at my words, forgetting all about what he's doing or where he's at. Never even sees the hit coming until it's too late. Rookie mistake number one is never to lose focus under any circumstances. He's the one who taught me that. Zane's fist connects with the side of his head, knocking him flat on his ass.

"Goddamn it, Ax!" Asher's eyes pin mine, and I'm sure anyone else would piss themselves from the intensity of it, but not me. He's been giving me the same damn look since I can remember.

"I win." Zane adjusts the mess of hair that's fallen out of his rubber band and reaches out a hand to help Asher to his feet.

Asher smacks it out of the way and gets up on his own. "Bullshit, he fucking handed that win to you."

Zane shrugs. "Still counts."

"Payback is a bitch, big brother." I blow a cloud of

smoke in his direction and twist my lips into a wide-ass grin.

"Put your money where your mouth is then, *little* brother." Asher holds his hands out to his side in a silent challenge. Blood drips down his chin from the hit he just took from Zane as the creases around his eyes tighten.

I let his words linger in the air between us for a few seconds. No use giving away all my cards just yet.

"Care to make a wager on this?" I stub out my cigarette and stroll onto the mat, keeping my steps slow and precise. Taunting him is just too damn easy. Too. Damn. Easy.

"What did you have in mind?" His eyebrows lift as his head tilts to the side, studying me, trying to get in my head. He needs to stop hanging around Zane so much because he is picking up on that shit, and I can't handle two of them.

I tilt my head to the side, pretending to weigh my options. "Simple. I win, you replace Willie Mae."

Asher crosses his arms over his chest and lets out a long exhale. "And *when* I win?" Never said my brother wasn't a cocky bastard.

"I'll take nightshift duty with Wildflower for a month." I know the exact second I have him. His features loosen as his eyes light up. That's as close to a smile as I'm going to get from him, and I'll take it.

"Deal." Asher jerks his chin at me. "Don't go crying like a fucking pussy to Charlee when you can't hack it, though."

"No promises. After all, she likes me better." I bounce on my feet against the mat, keeping him guessing.

He figures out what I'm doing and ignores me until I step foot in front of him with my hands up.

"We went to the barn earlier and had another discussion with your *friend*." Asher's body twists as his arm arcs out, trying to catch me off guard with that comment, and it almost works, too, but I manage to drop down and avoid his right hook seconds before it can connect with my jaw.

"Why the fuck didn't you wake me?" My fist moves forward, aimed at his stomach. They know better than to leave me out of this shit.

Asher drops his elbows, blocking the hit. "Figured you were busy, and Kelsey needed you more."

"Fair point." Sometimes, having Detective Asher make an appearance is worse than this brooding Asher. "He have anything interesting to say?"

"Not at first, but we eventually got him to talk," Zane adds from behind me, and there's no missing what he's implying. My shoulders tense at being robbed of the privilege myself.

"Relax, Ax. We didn't fucking kill him. Saved that honor for you." Asher must have read the look on my face.

"Good." The need to feel his bones crush underneath my hands fuels me on, and I toss a few more hard punches to Asher's face. He manages to dodge every one, but it doesn't stop me from trying harder.

"Found out some more info on Donnelly, but still not sure what the connection is to Kelsey's mom or why she had that tattoo. He has a few sons and a daughter, Kennedy," Asher says after a few more hits. "She's our way inside to figure out what the hell is going on."

"Great." A lump forms in my throat as images of

how I met Kelsey flood my head. I'm not sure I feel like having history repeat itself. "Because things didn't get fucked the last time I did that."

"Calm your shit. Zane's taking the point on this one." That settles my nerves some, but then he has to keep talking. "Also did some digging on social media and found out she'll be at Orphic tonight with some friends."

"You do remember what happened the last time either of us was there, right?" My gut twists into knots at the thought of going back there. It's been two years, but it doesn't mean that place isn't still my own special brand of hell. "It's the reason Kelsey was put in the line of fire in the first place, and last time you were there, it wasn't exactly a picnic either. Or have you forgotten?"

"I didn't forget." His face pales for a split second, no doubt reliving what he did to Charlee, before his features harden. "Charlee's forgiven me for that, but I'm not looking forward to going there either. Except we ain't got no choice right now. We thought it was just some asshole punks shooting at you before, and now that this shit is much more serious, we need to get ahead of it before it's too late. Think about what's at stake if we wait. Or, would you rather we tuck tail with our dicks between our legs and let them have a go at your girl?"

"Over my dead fucking body." All of my rage boils to the surface, extending into my fists. I nail Asher so hard he falls down onto the mat.

Instead of getting pissed like I expect, he rubs his lip, giving me a quick nod at the same time. "That's what I thought." He stands to his feet and walks to the corner of the room where Zane is standing, watching it all. I wait for the retaliation hit to come, but it never does. His eyes go to the phone that he's just grabbed off the table and then back to me. "Charlee's upstairs making breakfast, and Kelsey's with her." Without a backward glance, he heads upstairs, leaving Zane and me standing there with our dicks in our hands.

I'm wondering what the hell just happened and who that was because Asher's never let me off easy on anything in my life. Zane's eyes burn into the side of my face, and I whip my head in his direction. "What?" The blank look he's giving me is getting on my last damn nerve.

Zane watches me for a few more beats as his eyebrows pinch together. "You really don't know?"

"Wouldn't be asking if I did, Dr. Phil." I fight the urge to roll my eyes at him.

He pushes off the wall, shaking his head at me. "You're a dumbass. He fucking let you win."

"Bullshit." I cross my arms over my chest and hold Zane's stare.

"After everything he's been through, everything he's lost, Asher's all about family. If you really think he'd waste the chance to buy you another truck or that he'd give up even a moment with either one of his girls, then you don't know our brother at all." Zane jerks his chin in the direction Asher just went and rubs away some of the blood that's matted in his beard before he heads up the stairs, leaving me alone on the mat.

Everything he's said takes a few seconds to sink in, but when it does, I feel like the dumbass Zane called me. Bastard has always been too fucking perceptive for his own damn good, but still, he has a point. Then my brain catches up to what Asher said. Wildcat's awake, and after last night, my body's humming with the need to touch her. To make sure she's all right. I haul ass up the stairs, anxious to see her and hold her. Whether or not she'll let me is still up for debate. Good thing I enjoy a good fight.

21

KELSEY

My eyes are dry and swollen from crying all morning, but holding Lily is dulling some of the aches inside my chest. Her chubby little cheeks are the bright spot in an otherwise crappy morning. I don't even care that she's drooling all over my yellow camisole. The tips of my fingers brush along her soft skin as I coo at her. Those green eyes and dimples of hers ease the storm brewing inside of me, if only for a moment.

Asher and Zane are in the kitchen helping themselves to a cup of coffee and the mound of pancakes Charlee's cooking. When she cooks, her Mexican heritage comes through loud and clear. She makes enough food to feed an army. While it smells good, my stomach's in too many knots to even attempt food, and I don't even have a damn hangover to blame it on.

Movement from my side catches my attention, and I know who it is even before he speaks. "Smells good in here," Axel says to Charlee, but his gaze is fixed on me, and there's no missing the heat behind his eyes as he takes in the scene in front of him.

My body tenses up at the sound of his voice. Images of him holding me while I cried last night has my heart speeding up. I'm not sure where we stand now. Have I forgiven him for lying and using me as a way in to get to Charlee? Not completely, but I'm getting there. And that's a thought that has me on edge.

Where do we go from here?

He kisses the side of my head and whispers in my ear, just loud enough for me to hear. "How are you feeling, Wildcat?"

"I'm okay." My voice cracks, but I force as much strength into the words as I can.

"You sure?" His thumb traces the side of my face in small, soft circles, mimicking a similar motion to the one I was doing to Lily.

A flush rises to my cheeks as his gaze holds mine. It's soft and warm, different from the arrogant bastard I've forced myself to believe he is. His blue eyes deepen as they drop to Lily and back up to me. He kisses my temple while my eyes drop down to his gray sweats that are giving me an eyeful of his package. My throat goes dry as I remember how talented he is with that piece of equipment.

Lily's cries break me out of my trance, causing me to put all indecent thoughts aside. I rock her gently in my arms to soothe her, much like my mom used to do with me, and my heart breaks even more that I'll never feel her love ever again.

"I've got her." Asher takes her from me and props her over his shoulder as he rubs her back. His tattooed hand is so big it covers her little body. "Daddy's here, Lily pad."

I watch the whole thing unfold with my mouth hanging wide open.

"Don't worry. You get used to it," Axel whispers next to me, making me jump in my seat.

"Used to what?" My eyebrows pinch together, and I brush it off like I wasn't just caught staring at his brother like a crazy person.

"Seeing a scary fuck like him go soft like that with a baby." A smile flashes across his face as he leans in and plants another quick kiss on my mouth. The warmth of his touch lingers on my lips long after he pulls back, taking the open seat next to me. His fingers hook around my neck, massaging any tension away. He can't stop touching me, and I'm not afraid to admit that I love every bit of it.

Asher clears his throat a couple of times, gaining our attention. "Does the last name Donnelly mean anything to either one of you?" He glances between Charlee and me.

Charlee leans her hip against the counter and twists her lips to the side as she taps the corner of her mouth with a fingernail. "It might." She sinks her teeth into her bottom lip as she thinks harder.

A vague sense of familiarity comes over me as I rack my brain for a face or name. It isn't long before one pops into my head. "Didn't we go to school with a Kennedy Donnelly?"

"Yes! That's it." She snaps her fingers at me. "I think my dad did business with hers. She had, like, a handful of older brothers that were so hot." Charlee bounces on her feet as we laugh and fall into a trip down memory lane.

"Really, Charlee?" Asher makes a growl that comes from deep within his throat, but there's no malice in his tone.

"Well, I mean...they were *okay* looking." Charlee backtracks as red colors her cheeks.

Axel snorts and bends down until his lips brush against my ear. "How about you? Is that what you think, too, Wildcat?"

I shiver from the feel of his lips against the shell of my ear, and it takes everything I have to keep my voice coming out in a smooth, controlled tone. "Maybe."

The corners of his eyes crease as he lets out a laugh. "But we both know that I'm the better option, and I look forward to reminding you later who you belong to."

I squirm in my chair and squeeze my thighs together to keep from letting out a moan that's begging to be set free. Instead, I focus on the conversation at hand. "Why are y'all asking about the Donnellys?" My head bounces from brother to brother, suspicion replacing my Axel fog. It doesn't escape my attention that throughout this entire conversation, Zane has remained in the background as an observer. I can't tell if that makes him the smart brother or the scary one. My money is on a little of both.

"No reason." Axel rubs his thumb along his bottom lip and looks away from me.

"You are a terrible liar, Axel." I yank his thumb away from his lip and grab his face to make him look me in the eye. "You want me to trust you, to forgive you, then you need to start trusting me with the truth."

He presses his mouth together in a tight line,

working something out before he finally lets out a breath. "We have a lead on who might be responsible for..." His words drop off, but there's no need to finish. I know exactly what he was going to say.

"Then I'm coming with you." I sit up straighter in my chair as emotions threaten to overpower me.

"I am, too," Charlee adds as she flips the last pancake onto the plate.

"No way. I'm not letting you go anywhere near this shit after what happened last time." A vein pulses on the side of Asher's neck as he clenches his jaw, but he keeps his hold on Lily gentle. It seems my stubbornness is about to cause World War III.

"If you think I'm going to let her do this without my support, then you have another thing coming, Asher Deacon Savage." Charlee points her finger in his face as her green eyes blaze against her olive skin.

"Oh shit. She just middle-named you. You're in deep shit." Axel whistles, and that does it. I'm not letting him off the hook so easily this time.

"Says the guy whose initials are literally A-S-S, Axel Shawn Savage."

That wipes the grin from his face, but I manage to hear a deep chuckle off to my side. Apparently, Zane does have a sense of humor after all.

"If it involves me, then I'm coming with you. End of discussion." My tone brooks no further argument.

"Exactly," Charlee adds in the same stern tone. "And it'll be fine. I can have Mrs. Stapleton come watch Lily while we're gone," she rushes out in one long breath before Asher can stomp on her parade.

I wait, wondering if Asher's going to explode, but he must know that there's no arguing with her when her mind is made up because he just nods. "Fine, but you aren't out of my sight all night."

Axel stares at me, not saying a word, and that's almost worse than freaking out like Asher, but it's his rigid posture that has me on alert.

"What aren't you telling me?" A tingle of unease races up my spine.

"We're going to *Orphic*."

"Oh." Bile fills my throat at the thought of going back there. That place doesn't hold any good memories for me at all. It's where I met Axel, where I was kidnapped, and where everything turned to shit. Then I think back to images of my mother, how much I'm going to miss her, and how much of my life she's going to miss now because of the bastards that took her from me. It's enough to fuel my anger and push any reluctance away. "I'm still coming with you."

"Me too," Charlee adds.

"But—" Asher starts in, but she cuts him off.

"I told you I forgave you and Zane for taking me that night, and I'm still coming with you." She holds her head up high, making it clear she isn't budging on this.

"You sure?" Axel's hand rubs the back of my neck, pulling my attention back to him. The battle brewing behind his eyes tugs on my heartstrings. "I don't want it to..."

My finger rests against his lips, shushing him. The warmth of his skin is a comfort I feel down to my bones, and knowing he'll be there to have my back this time is all the encouragement I need. "I'll be fine."

"Okay." He tilts his forehead down against mine and sighs. "Promise me if it brings up old memories and you want to get out of there, you'll tell me."

"I promise."

Charlee claps her hands together, ignoring her brooding husband. "Date night."

I swallow down the lump in my throat and force myself to keep it together. There are many stages of grief. Last night, I had a good cry to let my emotions out. Now I'm angry and ready to make the bastards pay that took my mom from me.

22

AXEL

After our fun morning of arguing with the girls, the guys and I spent time coming up with a plan for tonight. It was the longest afternoon of my life. Spending it with my brothers was not how I envisioned today going. I wanted nothing more than to grab Kelsey, bury myself between her thighs all day long, and fuck our frustrations of this whole situation away. Much to my disappointment, she was with Charlee doing girly shit all damn day, not that she would let me near her anyway. I think it was also part of a tactic to avoid me and any chance of discussing what happened last night.

Now, we're at the bottom of the stairs waiting for our women, and Asher looks like he's ready to jump out of his skin. Zane's leaning against the wall without a care in the world. At least he finally did something with his fucking hair tonight.

"What is taking them so long?" Asher paces back and forth, tugging on the buttons of his dress shirt with the third cigarette he's had in the last thirty minutes hanging out of his mouth.

All three of us are dressed in dark button-down shirts and matching slacks. Not our choice, but we lost that vote when we let the women come along. My body is aching for a basic pair of jeans and a simple T-shirt right now.

"It can't be that hard to just throw some shit on and call it a day." Asher rubs a hand along his face.

"Clearly, you still know nothing about women." I chuckle and blow a cloud of smoke in his face.

He stops in his tracks and clenches his fists with an unspoken message. The meaning is clear as day. If we weren't going out tonight, then I'd be sporting one hell of a black eye and a fat lip. "I know plenty, dickhead. It shouldn't take this long."

"Tell ya what—why don't you go tell them that and let me know how that works out for you?" I point to the stairs, hoping he takes the bait. Nothing would make me happier than to see this.

Zane stays against the wall and doesn't say a word, but the knowing stare he gives me says enough. I'm right. Asher is wound way too fucking tight tonight.

A short while later we hear the sound of heels hitting the wooden floor on the stairs. Charlee comes around the corner wearing a short black dress that fits her like a second skin.

"What do you think?" She spins around, giving him a complete view, and the second he takes in the fact that the back barely goes to the top of her ass, his whole body tenses up.

"Charlee?" Asher's voice comes out strained as he

shoots her a look that would make most men shit themselves, but not Hellcat.

She meets his gaze head-on and doesn't back down. "Nope. Don't even say it. I finally got a sitter after months, and it's my night to have fun. You will not throw a fit about what I'm wearing and ruin it for me. I like it and think I look damn good, so deal with it."

Damn, I've got to hand it to Hellcat. She just handed my big brother his balls on a silver platter, and that was the best thing I've ever seen.

"That's the problem. You look too fucking beautiful, and I can't do what I need to do if I'm worried about protecting you from other assholes all night." Asher pleads his case one last time, but he should know better. Our women are stubborn as fuck and never take no for an answer.

"Good thing I'm prepared for that." She lifts the hem of the dress, revealing what would look like a garter belt to anyone else except for the pistol strapped to the outside of her thigh. "See." Her dark red lips spread into a wide-ass smile as she catches the looks on our faces. "And Kelsey has one too."

"Is it weird to be turned on right now?" Images of Wildcat with that strapped to her thigh have my mind reeling with all kinds of fun ideas for later.

"Shut up, Ax." Asher smacks me upside the head but doesn't take his eyes off Charlee. In a matter of seconds, a whole range of emotions fall across my big brother's face, from annoyance to reluctance to finally acceptance. He grabs her face and plants one on her in the middle of the living room. "I'm sorry for being an ass."

"It's okay. You're my ass, and I'll keep you." She toys with the buttons of his shirt and lightly taps his cheeks.

Kelsey's footsteps draw my eyes in the direction of the stairs, and I damn near swallow my tongue. A few stray red curls frame her face, drawing attention to the makeup on her face. Whatever dark shit she put around her eyes makes them pop even more, and the light pink on her lips only has me fighting the urge to suck on them.

My gaze travels down the rest of her, enjoying the view the whole way down. Her strapless emerald dress fits her like a second skin, leaving little to the imagination. Nude heels show off her long, lean legs. I will be deep inside her while she's wearing nothing but those later. The longer I stand here admiring the view, the more my dick strains against my zipper. All my blood is flowing south with one goal in mind, and if tonight weren't so important, I'd say to hell with it all to spend my night fucking her until she couldn't walk.

"You look sexy as fuck, Wildcat." I whistle. A blush colors her face, only making me crave her even more.

"Thanks." Her teeth dig into the bottom of her pink-stained lips as she returns the favor and takes in my appearance. Blue eyes darken the longer her gaze lingers on the seam of my slacks. I keep still, making sure she gets an eyeful of just how much I'm appreciating the view. "So do you."

A small thump echoes behind us, and Asher grunts.

"What was that for?" He rubs his shoulder.

"Why can't you be more like him when I dress nice?" Charlee shakes her head and storms off to her SUV, leaving him standing there with a frown on his face.

A few beats of silence pass by as he stares at the space she occupied seconds ago. "What did I do?"

"If I have to tell you that, Ash, then you have an even bigger problem." Zane plays with the ends of his beard, taking the whole scene in.

"Shit." The light bulb finally goes off, and he hauls ass out the door after his woman.

"I'm telling you, edible panties will go a long way in her forgiving you," I yell to his back and am given a middle finger as a response before he slams the door behind him.

Kelsey tilts her head to the side and furrows her brows together. "Edible panties?"

"It's sweet and sexy, thus making it the perfect gift." I reach out and interlock our fingers together, pulling her closer to me. The softness of her skin is a welcome contrast to mine. Mango fills the air between us. The sweetness makes my mouth water for a taste. I'm seconds away from saying *fuck it* and dragging her ass back upstairs, but then she smacks me on the side of the head and walks off, leaving me standing there with my dick in my hand.

"Idiot."

"What did I say?" My head whips in Zane's direction.

"I'll let you figure that one out all on your own, baby brother. Something tells me it'll be more fun to watch." He shakes his head and walks out the front door.

Every step is painful, but it's worth it if she's my prize at the end of the night.

Kelsey's whole body tenses the second we walk inside Orphic. The purple lights flicker, lighting up the crowded club, and for a weeknight, there are many more people here than I thought there would be. I'm sure it's only adding to her tension. It doesn't help that the last time she was here was when she was kidnapped.

My hand goes to the small of her back as I lean down and speak in her ear loud enough for her to hear me over the music. "You sure you're okay?"

She's frozen in place, taking the scenery all in. A sea of black furniture with splashes of purple trim lines the walkway. Aside from a few more tables, the place looks exactly the same. "I need a drink."

"That we can do." With a look, I send Zane off to get us some drinks. I'm sure he'll be coming back with a whole bottle of whiskey for himself.

The rest of us take over a table that's near the bar but gives us an open view of the dance floor and the back area where the restrooms are. After last time, we're leaving nothing to chance.

As I guessed, Zane comes back with some fruity shots for the girls, a Bud Light for me, and a bottle of whiskey for him and Asher. A few more rounds of drinks come and go, and the more alcohol Kelsey downs, the less tense she becomes. It isn't long before she and Charlee are itching to hit the dance floor. With a quick wave of a hand, they desert us, but the view is fantastic. That ass is mine later.

I lean back against the booth and take in more of the dance floor, which isn't that hard to see in this club lighting. A sea of bodies grind to some peppy dance song I don't know and don't care to know. Kelsey likes that shit, not me, and it's obvious by the way she and Charlee are smiling. Then, a certain face catches my attention.

"That her?" I lift my chin toward a group of girls that are dancing near ours, but it's the petite brunette that has my full attention.

Asher's eyes bounce from his phone and back to the group of girls. "Yup, that's her."

Toned pale legs lead up to a tight red, strapless silk dress as long dark hair hangs down her back, and blue eyes glisten from under a pair of black-rimmed glasses. "She's hot. Like sexy librarian type of hot."

"Ax." Zane kicks my leg under the table, making the beer bottles rattle together.

"Relax, Z. I have my own woman. I'm just saying you could do much worse than that." There's no stopping the smile that appears on my face. Zane needs this, and I'm only happy to do my baby brother's duty by giving him as much shit as possible.

"Explain to me why Axel isn't the one doing this again." He toys with the empty shot glass in front of him as he glares at Asher, but I'm the one who answers him.

"Because I took one for the team last time, and I'm still paying for that, asshole." I take a sip of beer and dare him to argue.

"You're the only one of us that's single." Asher cocks his head to the side as he, too, takes Kennedy in.

"That too," I smirk.

"Total bullshit," Zane grunts like a little bitch, and it only makes me want to goad him further.

"You know, getting laid might actually put you in a better mood," I say to him, but my eyes keep landing on Kelsey. She's bending and twisting her body in ways that have my head spinning with ideas for later, and judging by the way her eyes hold mine, she's doing it on purpose.

Next to me, Zane's face hardens, but there's no missing the way his eyes keep drifting in Kennedy's direction. He leans forward and scratches his beard. "How am I doing this then?"

"Let me put it in simpler terms for you. Hunter." I point to him with the tip of my bottle and then back to Kennedy. "Prey."

"Wiseass." Zane steals one of Asher's shots of whiskey and downs it. He's no doubt finding his balls to approach her.

As usual, Asher doesn't even acknowledge our bickering. "Wait until she goes to the bathroom and accidentally bump into her. If I have to guide you on what to do from there, then maybe I *should* send Axel in."

Zane shakes his head at us. "I can manage the rest from there, assholes."

"You sure? Need me to draw you a diagram of how shit works in case you've forgotten?" I press my mouth together to hide the grin that wants to break free.

"Fuck off, Ax." He clenches his jaw, but his eyes wander back over to the dance floor. His fingers toy with the ends of his beard as he continues to stare.

It isn't long after that Kennedy separates from her friends and heads toward the back of the club, where the bathrooms are.

"Showtime, Z." I nudge his foot with the same amount of force I was given earlier.

He pisses and moans the whole way, and like the good brothers we are, we watch the entire show with smiles on our faces.

Asher doesn't wait long for him to disappear from view before he starts in on me. "Care to explain to me what the fuck is going on with him?"

"Not my place, but know this—if there's anyone that he'll open up to about it, it's you, big brother." My thumb runs along the lip of my bottle as I lean against my elbows and meet Asher's stare head-on.

"Why's that?" Asher leans his weight deeper into the table.

"Because you know what it's like to be in prison." I'm doing my best to focus on our brotherly heart-to-heart, but it's difficult as hell when I catch sight of Kelsey running her hands along her body and swaying her hips my way. All of the blood in my body flows south, causing me to shift against the building pressure in my pants.

"Zane's never been locked up." His eyes narrow as he scratches the side of his head.

"Just because his cell doesn't have bars doesn't mean he isn't in one, big brother." Asher opens his mouth to argue, probably, but I'm done with this conversation. A certain redhead is all I can think about. I stand to my feet, shutting him up.

"This conversation isn't over, *little brother*," Asher mutters under his breath.

"Counting on it, Ash." I reach around and slap him on the shoulder as I head off to the dance floor. Wildcat has been sending me fuck-me eyes all night, and I can't stay away from her any longer. There's only so much a man can take. I come up behind her and pull her against me. The softness of her ass grinding against me has my dick twitching in appreciation. Oh yeah, tonight is going to get a lot better.

23
KELSEY

Familiar hands grip my waist before sliding down to squeeze my ass. "You better be shaking this just for me."

"Maybe. Maybe not." I bite back a smile as Charlee walks over to the table where Asher is to enjoy her man. Teasing him is proving to be too much fun tonight. "I'm still a single woman."

His lips suck on the lobe of my ear as he presses closer against me. "That right?"

"Yeah, that's right." We may have slept together, but we haven't hashed our shit out, and I'm not making this easy for him. He's never even apologized for deceiving me.

"I could fuck you right here on this floor and prove to everyone that you're mine. That what you want, Wildcat?"

"No," I groan, but the thought has wetness pooling between my thighs. Damn him for getting me all worked up like this.

"Liar. I feel your body trembling against mine." He moves my hair to the side with his chin and rests it against my shoulder. "I bet if I slid my fingers inside your panties, you'd be dripping for me."

I reach back and run my fingers through his short hair. "I'm not wearing any panties." I can give it back to Axel just as good as he's giving it to me.

Without another word, Axel spins me around and barrels toward the table so fast I stumble in my heels, but he catches me in time before I can face plant onto the club's dirty floor. "Y'all ready to head on home and call it a night?"

Asher's face is blank as he nods, but it's the look on Charlee's face that gives away how eager they are to leave as well.

They make it out the door just as a figure comes out from the shadows, blocking our exit.

"Well, if it ain't Axel Savage." The smell of tequila floats off his breath, stifling the air between us. His blonde hair is buzzed close to the scalp, revealing a few tattoos underneath. Dark eyes hold Axel's glare, and as he sways on his feet, he waves a finger in our faces. He's a few inches shorter than Axel and closer to my height, but you wouldn't know it by the way he's carrying himself.

Axel's grip on my hand tightens as his body tenses next to me. "Move, Neil." *So, he does know him.*

"Don't think so." He shoves Axel in the shoulder, but Axel's like a wall of stone and doesn't budge.

"Not the time, man." Axel's doing his best to keep calm on the outside, but a muscle in his cheek twitches, giving a glimpse of the storm brewing within. Things are going to go from bad to worse if I don't do something quick. My feet make to step past Neil when Axel's hand pulls me back against his side. The move is subtle, but it's enough to draw Neil's attention.

"Time don't mean dick anymore." Neil laughs as his lips twist into a cruel smile. "Now, ain't that funny. My sister's six feet under, and here you are walking around without a care in the fucking world with your new side piece. How's that for fucking fair?"

"Watch it." Axel's chest puffs up, and my eyes skirt past him, hoping Asher's brooding ass will come around the corner any minute to put a stop to this.

"What are you goin' to do if I don't, pretty boy? Kill me too?" A vein throbs in the side of his neck as he leans in.

Axel's nostrils flare at his words, and at the same time, all the air leaves my body. I couldn't have heard that right. He steps further into Neil's space until they're toe-to-toe. "Drunk or not, insult Kelsey again and I'll knock you the fuck out."

Neil's body coils up, ready to strike, when Asher's deep voice is like music to my ears. "Problem here?"

Neil spins around, tilting his head back until he meets Asher's gaze. "Nope. I was just leaving." He glances over his shoulder at Axel and points a finger at him. "Watch yourself, Savage. Big brother won't always be around to protect any of you." With that, he disappears just as fast as he appeared.

"Who was that?"

"No one." And just like that, he erases any thoughts I've had about trusting him.

"Charlee's waiting." Asher holds Axel's gaze, having an unspoken conversation.

I press my lips together to keep from saying something I'll regret and stomp off into Charlee's car.

The air inside the SUV is stifling with tension the whole way home. Axel doesn't even wait until the engine is off before he has me out and tossed over his shoulder.

"Later," he tosses out to Charlee and Asher but keeps his strides quick and purposeful all the way inside the house. He slams the door shut and slides me down his shoulder onto my feet.

It takes me a minute to steady myself, but when I do, I cross my arms over my chest and wait him out. "Ax, we need to talk about what happened tonight."

He grabs a remote off of the nearby table and hits a button like I never said a word. Music starts to fill the room. It only takes me a minute to recognize the song. "Hellfire" by Barns Courtney blares through the speakers, and heat rises in my cheeks.

He grabs a chair from the kitchen and drags it out into the middle of the living room. Gaze never wavering from mine, he sinks down into it and crooks a finger at me. There's no missing the glint behind those blue eyes, but then he flashes those damn dimples, and I can't resist no matter how irritated I am with him at the moment.

I close the distance between us until the tips of my heels are touching the tips of his boots. My eyes take him in, searching for any clues, but come up empty. He's up to something, and with Axel, you never know what that all entails.

"You like to shake your ass. You shake it for me and me alone." He sinks his teeth into his bottom lip and roams his hands over my body.

"Right here?" My head whips around the room, making sure no one else is around. It's just us in the middle of the living room in front of an open window. If it weren't for the fact that the place is surrounded by trees and cameras, I wouldn't even be considering it.

"Yup." He nods and rubs his thumb along his bottom lip. "Right here, right now."

"To this song?" My eyebrows pinch together as it dawns on me what his game is.

"*Only* to this song." His tongue darts out, licking his bottom lip as his chest heaves. He's doing his best to put on a brave front, but I can see his demons lurking beneath the surface. They may not be as dark as Zane's, but I'm going to dance with them nonetheless.

I get lost in the heaviness of the bass and let the lyrics roll off my body in a slow, seductive rhythm. My hips swivel and sway as I slide my hands up my body, letting my skirt lift a bit higher along the way, giving him just a taste, and squeezing my breasts. My fingers pinch and tease through the material of my dress until my nipples are stiff peaks.

Being back at Orphic brought up more memories and emotions from our past than I thought they would, but right now, there's only one piece of the puzzle I'm interested in solving.

I unzip my dress and peel it down my body, one slow inch at a time, and flick it in his direction with the tip of my shoe. Next, I slide the garter holding the gun down my leg and over my shoe before carefully setting it on the couch behind me. I'm in nothing but my nude heels, and it's so damn freeing.

Axel sinks deeper into his chair, but there's no

missing the way his chest is rising and falling in rapid succession. They say sex is power. Right now, Axel is eye fucking me like a man starved, and I'm his next meal. I believe it. He just handed me the keys to his kingdom, and this queen is going to teach him what it means when you fuck with her. Time to turn the tables on him. To show him what it's like to be at someone else's mercy for a change.

My eyes dance around the room, looking for something, when they land on the buckle of his belt, and an idea sparks to life. I stroll forward, dragging out my steps and giving him time to admire this view because he's going to be too pissed later to touch me.

I unbutton his shirt, revealing his ripped chest, and push the shirt halfway down his shoulders. My tongue licks along the outlines of the skull tattoo that's drawn on his chest right over his heart as my hands move down to unbuckle his belt and slide it out of the waistband of his pants, letting the leather slip between my fingers.

"What are you doing with that?" He cocks his head at me.

"I want to play too." I run the fingernails of my free hand along his bare chest and tilt my head, staring at him with wide, innocent eyes.

"What did you have in mind?" The muscles in his throat flex as he watches me and twists a lock of my hair around his finger.

I clasp my fingers around his wrist and pull both of his hands behind his back. "This."

He lets me bind his wrists behind him and to the chair. Next are his pants. I pull them and his boxer briefs down. Axel lifts his hips to help me get them down to just below his ass, and my mouth waters at the sight. His massive cock stands at full attention, glistening with precum, begging me to taste it.

I slip my heels off and get on my knees in front of him. My left hand rests on his thigh as I stroke him with a firm stroke with my right one.

He lets out a low hiss that I feel down to my core. I wrap my lips around him and suck. My tongue darts out, playing with the tip of his head. Salt and Axel fill my mouth, and it's a flavor I've missed. Such a shame I'm playing dirty tonight. Otherwise, I'd love to finish this.

His hands strain against the belt as he thrusts his hips up to meet my mouth. I hollow out my cheeks and keep at him, sucking and licking his length, until I feel him begin to throb. I pull back, letting his dick slip out of my mouth, and stand up.

"Why did you stop?"

I stretch my hands to either side of the chair and bend over until my lips are hovering above his, close enough to feel the heat of his breath, but that's as far as I go.

"That was fun." I turn my back on him and haul ass toward the stairs, giving him a view of my naked back the whole way.

"Fuuuuuck! Where the hell are you going?" The chair creaks from the weight of him struggling. That belt won't hold him long, so I power walk up the stairs, grabbing my gun and garter along the way. The last thing I want is for someone to get hurt because of my carelessness.

"Good night, Ax." I toss over my shoulder and hear him mumbling expletives behind me.

"Wildcat, get back here right now."

I wipe the sides of my mouth and disappear around the corner into my room. This round goes to me. I just hope it gets him to talk.

24
AXEL

Fire pumps through my veins as I watch her naked ass jiggle up the stairs. She left me here with my dick out and hard as a fucking rock, still glistening with her spit. My balls ache in need of release. After seeing Neil tonight, I needed to forget that part of my past and get lost in her, but then she fucked me even more. I just wish it was in the literal sense.

The front door bursts open, and heavy steps hit the wooden floors, bringing me out of my head. "What the fuck, Ax? I don't want to see that shit." Asher jumps back like the sight of my dick frightens him.

"Shut the hell up and get me out of this." I'm not in the mood to give him shit about knocking first because all my focus is on a certain redheaded devil whose ass is going to be fucked so hard when I catch her.

"Hold still." He bitches and moans the whole time he works the belt. Whatever Wildcat did, the fucker is on there pretty good.

The leather loosens, and I tug it free the rest of the

way. I pull my pants up, doing my best to tuck my aching dick away, and get to my feet.

"Ax!"

"Don't worry, Ash. Everything's fine." I wave him off and storm up the stairs. My shirt catches on the railing, so I tear the fucker off and toss it behind me. I've never been so pissed and turned on all at once. It'll be a miracle if Wildcat can walk when I'm through with her.

Her door's shut, but that ain't going to keep me out. Besides, it locks from the outside. Not sure what she was thinking on that part.

I barrel into the room like a storm, ready to rain down on her naked ass. She takes one look at me and runs to the bathroom, attempting to shut the door in my face.

"Oh no you don't." I push it back open hard enough to let me in, but not hard enough to hit her with it. No matter how pissed I am, I'd never ever hurt her like that.

She cowers down for a brief second. Then, as if a switch is flipped and she realizes what she's doing, her spine stiffens as she stands taller and glares at me.

"What the hell was that for?" It takes everything I have to keep my focus on her and not her gorgeous-as-fuck body that's on full display for me or her tits rising and falling with every heavy breath she takes.

"You deserved it. To see what it's like to be played with like you don't matter. To be locked in a fucking cage like you're a damn toy." Color flushes her face the more words she throws at me, and I wish it was for an entirely different reason. A stray strand of red curls falls in her face as her tits move with every deep breath she takes. I want nothing more than to suck them into my mouth, but I clench my fists and refrain from touching her just yet. Something tells me she'd go feral if I came anywhere near her right now.

"Is that what you think?" A lump forms in my throat at her words.

"Yes. No. I don't know." Her voice shakes as she loses some of her bravado, sinking closer against the tile wall.

I close the rest of the distance between us and put my hands on her shoulders, moving my thumbs in small circles on the sides of her pale neck. She flinches at the contact, but I ignore it and keep all my attention on her. "Look at me."

She sighs and slowly lifts her head to meet my gaze. The hurt I see behind them is like a swift kick in the balls. I thought I was getting through to her after I held her the other night, but the truth is I was a pussy that never gave her the one thing she needed. To hear the actual words from me.

"You matter. You matter more than anyone in my fucking life."

"Just not enough to hear the truth from you about tonight, right?" Tears pool in her eyes, and all thoughts of her naked body fade away as a crushing ache hits me in the chest.

My hands drop, and I back away, putting some distance between us. "I've been trying so hard to get you to forgive me that the last thing I want to do is tell you something else that'll make you think of me as an even bigger piece of shit."

"Then start by trusting me with the truth." She folds her arms across her chest and schools her features.

I rub my hand over my face and sigh. I'm about to cut open my chest and hand her my heart on a silver platter. I just hope she doesn't end up crushing it. "Her name was Mary Stevens. We were fourteen when we met. She was the new kid who transferred in the middle of our freshman year. From the day I punched Daniel Hastings in the face for calling her trash, we became friends, close friends. Things were fine between us. Then shit changed at the beginning of our senior year." My voice cracks as visions of her dark eyes and long blonde hair flash through my mind. She always did look like Neil's fucking twin.

"What happened your senior year?"

"Wildcat, you don't want to hear this."

"Tell me what happened." Her jaw clenches as her gaze burns into mine.

"She told me she had feelings for me, and like an idiot, I told her the truth of how I felt. I didn't think of her that way. She was my friend, nothing more. It didn't help that while we were friends, I had lots of girls." That's the best way I can put it to her without sounding like the immature bastard I was back then. "We were at a party and fought before she stormed off in her car. That was the last time I saw her. The next morning, I found out from Zane that she was hit head-on by a drunk driver and was killed instantly."

Her jaw drops, and as soon as I say the words, I want to swallow them back down, but I suck it up and force the rest of the shit out.

"Everyone knew we had a fight that night and that I'm the reason she got behind the wheel angry. Instead of being her friend and protecting her, I was blowing off steam with some random hookup at the party."

"It wasn't your fault, Ax. You were just a kid."

"A dumb kid."

"Thank you for telling me." Her body sinks further against the counter as all the tension leaves her.

"Now you know why I locked you in here that night to keep you safe." I close the distance until we're toe-to-toe. My hands itch with the need to touch her. To make sure she's still here. In front of me. "Everything I do is to protect you. I can't lose another person I care about. I can't. After that night, I swore to myself I'd never let anyone take you or hurt you again, and I'm the dumbest prick of all. Because that's all I've been doing, but that stops now."

"Yeah?" Her blue eyes glisten with more tears, making me feel like the biggest ass on the planet.

"Yeah." I press my forehead to hers, letting her mango scent fill me. "I'm sorry that you ever thought you weren't worth more because you are everything to me." I let out a heavy sigh as I pull back and cup her face.

"I'm sorry, too, for leaving you..." This time when her face heats, it's damn well for the right reasons as she gestures down to my undone pants.

"With my dick out?" My lips twitch, but I fight to keep the smile off my face. Something tells me if I did that right now, she'd kick me in my nuts.

Her eyes dip down to my mouth and back up to me. I know what she wants just by that simple look. I lean down and meet her the rest of the way, crushing my mouth to hers. Her tits press up against my chest, wreaking havoc on my balls.

My tongue teases at the seam of her lips until she opens up for me, letting me inside. The warmth of her mouth is like coming home after a cold, hard day. I suck on her tongue, enjoying the taste of us mixed together.

Her full lips meld with mine. Taking and giving all at the same time, but it's not enough. It'll never be enough. I need more. I'll always need more.

I lick at the column of her throat, enjoying the taste of her skin and the way her moans vibrate against it. I can't resist sinking my teeth into the pulse point on her neck. Her body trembles the harder I bite down as her fingers dig into the sides of my head, bringing me as close as she can. It makes my dick twitch.

My fingers slide up the side of her body, stopping at her tits. They fill my hands perfectly. The palms of my hands massage and rub the soft flesh until she's writhing against the counter, begging me for more. I take turns sucking each of her dusty pink nipples in my mouth, flicking with my tongue until they're stiff peaks.

I break the kiss before I come in my pants like a damn teenager and press my forehead to hers. The heat of our breaths becomes one as every muscle in my body aches to fuck her.

"Why did you stop?"

"Finally, getting my fucking dessert." I grip her ass and lift her onto the bathroom counter. The moment the cold tiles touch her skin, she lets out a small gasp, but I never stop. All this shit from the past has my body on adrenaline overload. I know what I'm starving for, and that's what I'm going to get.

I kiss my way down her body, kneeling on the floor between her legs. The tile bites into my knees, but I'd stay like this forever if I could. I grab her ankles and plant the heels of her feet against my shoulders. My thumbs spread her open, exposing all of her to me. "You're so fucking gorgeous. Pink and wet, just for me."

The tip of my nose rubs along her inner thigh as my

fingers dig deeper into the cheeks of her ass. My tongue slides up and down her slit, enjoying the taste of her exploding in my mouth. "And baby, you taste like paradise—tropical and sweet."

My lips wrap around her clit once more, sucking and biting as two of my fingers thrust inside her. The pad of my tongue flicks against her clit in rhythm with my hand, making her thighs tremble. "You're so fucking wet. My good girl, that's dirty just for me."

"Don't stop."

I blow on her clit as my fingers continue to sink into her, bringing her to the edge of sanity. After a few more strokes, she clamps down on my fingers.

She lets out a mumbled moan as her inner walls milk my fingers. "I need you, Ax. Please."

"What do you want?" I suck on her clit hard enough that her hips buck up off the counter. "Tell me, and it's yours, Wildcat."

"I want you inside me." Her hooded eyes and flushed face are one hell of a fantasy brought to life.

I stroke my dick, watching her teeth sink into her bottom lip the way I'm planning on sinking into her, but not until she understands this is permanent. "Are you sure you want this, Wildcat? Because there's no going back from here. Only forward."

"I'm sure."

My hands wrap around her thighs and pull her closer to the edge until her ass hangs off a bit. I align myself against her slit, grip her waist with my other hand, and bury my dick inside her with one quick thrust that has tingles of warmth spreading from my chest down to my balls.

"You're mine. And you're never leaving me again. We

fight, then we'll fuck it out until we're too exhausted to remember why we're mad in the first place." My hips thrust in and out, hitting her so deep I don't know where I end and she begins.

"Please?" Her core clenches around me as her fingernails scratch along my back the harder I slam into her, and it's fucking hot.

"That's it, Wildcat. I'm yours. Mark me. Fuck me just like that." I glance down and watch the space where we connect. Watching as I disappear inside of her is hot as fuck.

A few more deep-seated thrusts and her inner walls clench around me as another orgasm tears through her. I pump into her even faster until tingling at the base of my spine spreads into the lower half of my body. A few more strokes are all I can manage before my dick twitches, spilling inside her.

We sag against the counter, catching our breath, as she runs her nails along my back and lets out a small purr.

"What now?"

I pull back but make no move to separate us. "Now, I'm going to punish you. How does death by orgasm sound?"

She laughs as I wrap her legs around my waist and carry her out of the bathroom straight to the mattress, where she lands with a small laugh, and I get to work making good on my promise until she's passed out next to me.

I bury my nose in her mess of red curls, inhaling her mango scent that now smells like a mixture of the both of us. "There will never be anyone else because, Wildcat, you're it for me. You were never a game, and you are my favorite toy. One I want to play with forever," I whisper against the side of her head as I pull her sleeping form tighter against me and drift off, too.

Tonight we were able to forget all of the bullshit swirling around us and enjoy each other, but come tomorrow, I'll make every bastard regret the day they fucked with us.

25

KELSEY

Music vibrates through my chest the closer I get to the front door. There's a bit of a bigger crowd than usual, but at least the line is moving rather quickly. I need the distraction tonight. Men suck. Well, at the moment just one dickhead in particular has my heart aching.

I'm almost to the front, near the door, when everything happens so fast. One minute, I'm bracing to forget about my troubles, and the next, tires squeal. Arms grab me from behind, and I'm shoved inside a van.

My chest is crushed against a musty carpet as I'm pinned down between a hard body and the floor. An engine rumbles beneath my body when I feel it turn. I open my mouth to scream, but a hand slams over it, trapping any sound inside. I will not give up. I do, and I'm dead. My knees dig into the floor as I attempt to push against the body on top of me, but it's like trying to move a wall. They don't budge.

Warmth creeps along the flesh of my neck the closer his mouth gets to my ear. "Keep fighting me, Chiquita. I like it." He digs his groin into my ass, letting me know just how *much he really does. Hands slide over my body, squeezing my breasts as I do my best not to hyperventilate.*

"No!" My heart pounds against my chest as I sit up in a cold sweat. The stench of his cologne lingers in the air, making my stomach roll. That bastard is dead and buried, where he belongs, but he's still taunting me from the grave.

I wipe at the sweat beading on my forehead and reach over to Axel's side of the bed, finding it empty and cold. My fingers make contact with a small piece of paper, and my heart flutters in a different way as I read the note he left.

Morning, Wildcat,

Come eat, so after, I can eat you ;)

A smile appears on my face. Food is much needed after the wild night we had. I shake off my nightmare and push all thoughts of that horrible night back into the deep recesses of my mind. I throw on Axel's T-shirt and head downstairs to find him fast at work in the kitchen, shirtless. I lean a hip against the counter a short distance away from him and take in the view.

Gray sweats hang low enough on his waist to show off the toned definition of his back and give me one hell of a view of the outline of his firm ass. The muscles of his arms flex, moving his tattoos as he stirs the food.

"Hungry?" The sound of his voice has my face whipping up to find a shit-eating grin on his.

Heat rises to my cheeks at being caught. "Starving." *Not just for food.* I swallow the dryness in my throat and clench my thighs together to keep from jumping him right where he stands.

As if he can read my thoughts, his blue eyes darken and dip down to my chest. "You look good in my clothes,

Wildcat." He closes the short distance between us and sinks his teeth into my bottom lip. "But having you smell like me is even better." His hand cups my face, bringing my mouth to his. Our lips crush together, and the second I open my mouth, he wastes no time slipping his tongue inside. Axel kisses like he fucks—gentle and demanding—with a skilled precision I feel down to my core. His other hand slaps down on my ass before grabbing a handful, and the move is so primal it has a groan slipping out of me.

A slamming of the front door has us breaking the kiss, but Axel doesn't take his hand off my backside as he turns us toward the doorway.

Zane stumbles in wearing the same clothes from last night. His black button-up shirt hangs open, revealing his tatted-up torso and rock-hard abs. The rest of him is quite the sight to take in. His hair hangs down in a wild mess around his shoulders. If I didn't know any better, I'd say he has sex hair.

"Morning, Sunshine." Axel grins so wide it lights up his whole face the more of Zane's appearance he takes in. "Rough night?" His hand massages my ass, but he never takes his focus off of his brother.

Axel's hand works my body into a frenzy of need, and I bite on my bottom lip to keep quiet. The last thing I want to do is let out a moan in front of Zane.

Zane holds Axel's stare as the two of them do that brother smackdown they do with their eyes. "Not in the mood, Ax." His voice grates out like gravel. He runs a hand through his hair and shakes his head.

"You come home like that, and I'm not supposed to say anything?" Axel cocks a dark eyebrow at his brother, saying all he needs to with that one look.

Zane's posture stiffens. He looks calm on the outside, but appearances can be deceiving. The vein on the side of his temple throbs, serving as a warning to any sane person to back off, but Axel does what he always does and barrels right past that line, pushing until Zane has no other choice but to react.

"Welcome to the dark side, Z. Tastes good, don't it?" Axel licks his lips, and my thighs tremble, remembering how well that tongue worked me over last night.

Zane opens his mouth when a shrill scream pierces the air. The sound has the hairs at the back of my neck standing on end. At the same time, all humor is wiped from Axel's face. My stomach drops at their sudden change in mood. This is bad. Very bad.

Both of the brothers run out the door, but not before Axel shouts over his shoulder at me, "Wildcat, stay here."

As if that's happening. He should know better. I never do what I'm told. I follow out the door right behind them, and what we find has the coffee in my stomach wanting to come back up.

Asher's rubbing a crying Charlee's back as he shoots all three of us a look that has my veins turning to ice. His gaze darts from me in Axel's T-shirt to Zane's disheveled appearance. Unlike Axel, he doesn't say a word about any of it. That's not Asher's style. He observes but doesn't shoot off at the mouth unless he needs to.

"Who the hell is that?" Charlee's words fall on deaf ears. All three brothers seem to be having a silent conversation that Charlee and I aren't privy to. My attention is too focused on the dead body at their doorstep to give them hell about it right now.

The pulse in my throat races as I take in the trail of blood that flows down his mangled face, covering his entire chest. Whoever this guy was, they tortured him pretty bad before they killed him. There's not a recognizable feature on him, and then my eyes land on an important one. One that flicks a memory to life inside my head. His mustache. Not just any mustache either.

"Is that the creepy guy from the bar?" My voice comes out higher than intended, but I'm doing my best to keep from losing it. There's no way this can be happening right now.

"It is." Axel nods but doesn't take his eyes off the lifeless lump as Zane bends down and picks up the phone that's resting on the guy's chest. "How the hell did they get past our security or our fucking cameras, Ash?" A vein throbs on the side of Axel's neck the longer he stares at his brother. All traces of his usual laid-back demeanor are gone. In its place is one I've only seen on Asher's face. Something dark and deadly.

"I don't know, but I'm going to find out." Asher's whole body tenses as he squeezes Charlee tighter against his chest.

The phone in Zane's hand starts going off, and I feel like all the oxygen is being sucked out in a huge vortex. His eyes dip down to the screen as it lights up with an incoming text. "Well, looks like we can ask him ourselves. He wants a meeting."

"When?" Axel asks, throwing an arm around my shoulder and tucking me in against his side. The beat of his heart pounds erratically against my ear, causing me to constrict around him tighter.

"Tonight." Zane's Adam's apple moves as he visibly swallows.

My hands push off Axel's chest enough for me to meet his eyes. "I'm coming with you."

Axel shakes his head before I finish my sentence. "No way."

"Ax—"

"Remember when I told you last night you're mine, and I'll do whatever I need to in order to make sure you're safe, and you agreed to let me?"

I nod, knowing where this is going but hating that he has a damn point.

His forehead presses against mine. "This is one of those times, Kelsey, that I'm begging you to trust me." The tone of his words hits me square in the chest.

I know what he's really asking. Do I trust *him* enough with all of me? I know the answer to that without even blinking. With all the shit we've been through, the one thing he's always done without fail is protect me.

I nod. "Okay."

All tension leaves his body at that one word, and I sink against him, knowing somehow he'll make everything right or die trying.

26

AXEL

I can't shake the feeling that's crawling around inside my chest. I've been itching inside to crawl out of my skin the second we left the girls at home tonight. Something isn't sitting right with me. I have a bad feeling when we leave here, shit is going to be much different, and I'm not sure if it'll be for the better or worse.

Neither Asher nor Zane has said a word from the second we pulled into the driveway to the time we walked up to the lighted walkway and to the front door. They're both lost in their heads—for different reasons.

"Keep your shit together until we get out of here, Ax," Asher orders under his breath as he lifts his hand to knock.

"No promises." I keep my eyes straight ahead, burning a hole through the white wooden door.

Zane stiffens next to me, and I brace, knowing he's about to jump my shit as well, but before he can even open his mouth, the door opens.

A huge bald fucker with a Glasgow smile scarring

over his cheeks glares at us. He's a couple of inches shorter and has an SMG slung over his shoulder that I'm sure makes him think he's got the biggest dick in the room, and that makes my fingers itch to grab the 9mm I have strapped to my back.

Without a word, he steps back and lets us inside. The second my feet hit the hardwood flooring, I'm swallowed up by the massive interior. Everything is an ivory color with green accents inside. Very modern and simple. Nothing at all I would expect from an Irish mobster, but what the fuck do I know about decorating and shit?

A boy, who looks like his balls have barely dropped, comes around the corner wearing a black fedora. The blue of his eyes light up against his baby face the second he sees us.

"You're here. Name's Teegan." His eyes bounce between the three of us as he waits us out.

"Axel." I point to my brothers and do the introductions because I know they won't. "That's Asher, and the one with the hair is Zane." A sharp pain, no doubt from Zane's elbow, hits me in the lower back, but I ignore it. At least I know Zane is listening.

With a slight tilt of the head, he waves us inside. "Follow me." He takes off down the hall, knowing damn well that we're going to follow. I just hope we haven't entered the lion's den for a slaughter.

I stare at the back of his buzzed head that's peeking out from underneath his hat the entire flight of stairs until we're standing at an oversized door. One thing I'll say about Finn is that he's consistent. The house is done up in the same green and ivory color stuff all throughout.

It's so quiet when we enter the room, you can hear a pin drop. The three of us walk in with our eyes open and our mouths shut. We're not taking any chances of being taken by surprise.

My eyes do a quick glance at our surroundings, stopping on the younger guy who's sitting on a nearby sofa. He's the mirror image of the one we've been following. Only difference is he's wearing a black fedora with a red feather on it. I do a double-take a few times. Twins. Of fucking course. There's not even a mole or a fucking freckle to tell them apart.

"Took you long enough, fecker." The one on the sofa snickers at Teegan.

"Feck off, Keegan."

"Lads." That one word cuts through the air in warning, and that's all Finn needs to bring them in line.

"Sorry, Dad." Keegan dips his head toward the floor and sags back against the sofa, as the one that I know is Teegan stands next to Finn's desk like a guard dog. Well, more like a guard puppy.

While he reprimands his sons, we move closer, directly into his line of sight. I use this distraction as an opportunity to size him up. He's polished. Dressed from head to toe in a black suit that still has creases from being pressed. His salt-and-pepper hair is combed back in a neat style. There are a few similar characteristics to the boys in front of us, but he is more of an older version of his daughter. She's definitely better looking.

"Thank ye fer coming. I—"

A soft knock on the door cuts him off mid-sentence, and the one he referred to as Keegan opens the door.

"Oh, I'm sorry. I didn't mean to bother you. I thought you were done for the night. I can come back later." Her voice carries through the room on a soft breeze, and I feel Zane tense beside me. He better keep his shit together because the last thing we need is for Finn to find out what he did last night.

"Nonsense, *a stóirín*." Finn waves her forward. "Ye're never a bother. I always have time for me favorite *daughter*." I'm pretty sure that last bit is said mostly as a warning to us. Little does he know it's too little, too late for that.

Kennedy's heels echo against the wooden flooring. Each step she takes is like a hammer dropping down, reminding us that we're on borrowed time. In a matter of seconds, she could blow all this shit sky high. Asher stands still as a statue, projecting an air of indifference, but I can feel his temper brewing under the surface. Where I'm a loose cannon, he's more like a cobra taking it all in and striking when you least expect it.

My attention switches to Kennedy. A black pencil skirt wraps around her like a second skin as her green satin top is tucked in, making her look every bit the naughty librarian I pegged her as the night before. Her steps never falter as she comes around the desk.

Blue eyes, similar to Finn's, widen behind the thick black rims of her glasses the second she sees us. A shade of light pink tints the pale skin of her cheeks as a flicker of emotions flash across her face before settling into a blank stare, making me feel like a dick for what we had Zane do. She composes herself just as fast and focuses all her attention on Finn. Like father, like daughter.

"I need you to sign these so that I can send the reports to the bank first thing in the morning." There's no missing the slight waver in her voice. Her hands tremble at her sides as she waits for him to sign the documents, and I'm not sure if she's going to burst into tears or throw up.

"Shit," I mumble under my breath. Things have just gotten a bit more complicated for all of us. My gaze flicks to Zane, and he's gone stone cold, with his blank stare focused solely on her.

"Are ye feeling all right, Ken?" Finn's dark eyebrows pinch together as he studies her.

"I think I'm coming down with something. I'm going to head home after I fax this." She holds up the papers against her chest as her eyes skitter across the room, landing anywhere but on Zane. Every second that she's in here is another I can feel Zane slipping closer to the edge of insanity. He's wound up like a bomb ready to explode, and I just hope we can get him out of here before that happens.

"Ye want Molly to make ye some soup?" Finn puts a hand on her shoulders, and out of the corner of my eye, I see Zane clench his fists. Something tells me we're moments away from having a first-class seat to a giant shitshow.

"No. I'll be fine, Dad." She clears her throat and power walks toward the door without a backward glance.

I chance another look at Zane in my peripheral, but his gaze is plastered on Kennedy's retreating back as his chest heaves up and down. There's a slight flicker of emotion behind his eyes, but it fades just as quickly back into his cold, blank stare when he turns back around.

Finn opens his mouth to say something more, but Keegan beats him to it.

"I've got her." He jumps up from the couch, tips the end of his fedora at us, and follows out the door behind her.

"Thanks, Keeg. Days like these, I miss me wife." As if realizing what he's let slip, Finn changes the subject. "Now, where were we?" He leans back in his chair, but I feel the tension radiating off of him. There's a story there, but I'm not digging any deeper into that right now. I have more pressing matters to be concerned with at the moment.

I can feel Teegan's stare burning in our direction. When I cast a quick glance his way, his head is cocked to the side, studying Zane as his gaze flickers from him to the doorway Kennedy just fled through. His mind is beginning to put pieces of this fucked-up puzzle together. Not good for us at all. We need to hurry and rush things along, or we're going to be in the middle of a war zone soon. I drag my eyes back over to Finn and let out a small breath. I relax my shoulders and watch Asher question Finn.

"You were about to tell us why you left a dead body on my front porch." Asher crosses his arms over his chest and stands up taller, getting to the point. He's hanging on by a thread, and if Finn doesn't cooperate, he's going to snap. He just better keep his shit together until after I get answers of my own.

"Consider it an early gift." His lips curve into a wide smile around the edges of his cigar.

"Most people just send a card." Two can play this game. "And why are you so interested in my woman?"

"Let's call it a family matter." He shrugs and holds out a wooden box toward us. "Cuban?"

A vein throbs in the side of my neck, and a slight

shake of the head is all I can manage in response. I don't like being toyed with.

He shrugs, slides the tip through a small silver cutter, and clamps down. The snap echoes against the small space, causing me to place my hands in front of my nuts. Finn flicks open his lighter and takes a few puffs, savoring the cigar like we aren't in the room. It's all for show and grating on my last nerve.

"We are not family."

He leans back in his chair as his lips spread into a smile against the edges of the cigar. "Aren't we?"

I lean a step forward, ready to slam my fists down on his desk, when an elbow to the side knocks me back to reason. "We don't have time for games, so just spit out whatever bullshit you need to say so I can get on with finding these pricks and doing what I need to do."

He doesn't answer right away, just bounces his eyes between me and my brothers, stretching out the tension and letting us know our place in this meeting.

It's a waste of time. Pissing contests are nothing new for me. I hold my ground and wait him out. Intimidation doesn't work on me. I call two of the scariest motherfuckers I've ever met "brother," so he needs to try a bit harder next time.

This standoff lasts a few beats longer, and I'm not sure who breaks it first, but it doesn't matter. At least we're back to business.

"I like ye, Savage. Ye've got some balls on ye. I'll give ye that." He lifts a folder off his desk between two fingers and extends it out to me.

My thumb flips through the images the moment it's in my grasp, and a fire builds deep within my gut. Images of Kelsey and us reflect back at me. Some are from as far back as a couple of years ago. I grind my molars so hard they crack. "Why the fuck do you have these?"

"I protect me family." He rolls the cigar between his fingers and cocks his head to the side like that explains it all. This meeting has me itching to light one up myself, and I will as soon as we get out of here.

"You keep saying that. What the fuck are you talking about?"

"Still, I'm not sure ye are good enough for her." He keeps on babbling, lost in thought, but the rest of it is drowned out by the blood pumping in my ears.

My spine stiffens, and I have to count back from ten; otherwise, I'm going to beat my brother's ass right here. He kept something from us, and that's not how we do things. The second we get out of here, he'll be giving us answers. For now, my anger is directed at the Irish fuck in front of us.

"Out with it, Donnelly." There's no missing the unnamed threat in my words.

"I want to help you avenge the death of me sister."

"Your sister?" A lump forms in my throat as shit starts to make sense.

"Our mother had the same Celtic butterfly tattoo as her. All the women in our family do." His eyes pierce into mine with every word he says.

"No fucking way. That would make Kelsey your—"

"Niece." A smug smile creeps on his face. It takes everything I have to stay where I am and not wipe it off with my fist.

"Bullshit. You're lying." He has to be. Muscles in my body tense with every heavy breath I take.

"I promise ye I am not. With me sister marrying that

fecking idiot, we decided it was best to keep the fact that we're kin a secret, but I was never far away." He swipes a framed photo off of his desk and holds it out to me. "I've been watching her her whole life."

My throat goes dry as I stare down at the two babies sitting on a younger Finn's lap. One has dark hair and pale skin, but other than some chubby cheeks, Kennedy looks pretty much the same. Then I take in the second baby, and there's no mistaking those wild red curls that stick out on her head.

"Son of a bitch."

"That's Uncle Finn to ye." The smug bastard winks and leans back in his chair.

Turns out I was right. Things have just gotten more fucked.

27
KELSEY

Wet lips meet my shoulder, and at the same time, an arm cradles against my side, caging me in a cocoon of warmth. I blink the sleep from my eyes to find the outline of Axel staring down at me. He's lost in the shadow of darkness that blankets the room, but I'd recognize the scent of tobacco and cedarwood anywhere.

"You're back." I roll over onto my back and stare up at him. A smile he can't see spread across my face. "How did your meeting go?"

He sighs against my shoulder and changes the subject, something that doesn't go unnoticed, and I will be getting to the bottom of it later. "What are you doing in here?" His voice comes out low and smooth, melting my insides, like a fine Tennessee whiskey, as a thumb lightly strokes the side of my cheek.

"I couldn't sleep." It sounds stupid saying that out loud.

"So you came in here?" His lips smile against my skin.

"It felt safe." I shrug a shoulder, rethinking how lame I must sound, but if I tell him the truth, that'll lead to a whole other conversation. One I'm not ready for just yet.

He dips his head to mine and lets out a heavy breath. Something's off. His body is riddled with tension.

My hands come up to rub small circles into the space between his shoulders, feeling the muscles begin to relax under my touch. "Axel, is everything okay?"

His nose rubs against mine. "I need you."

Three simple words that hit me to the core. All the running I do would never erase these feelings he invokes within me, and I was foolish to think that by running, I could ever escape them or even want to.

"You have me. All of me." As soon as the words are out of my mouth, I know them to be true down to my soul. He owns every inch of me.

The hand stroking my cheek stills as I feel him gaze into my eyes through the darkness. His lips crush against mine in a bruising kiss. One that sets a trail of fire blazing through my body, dominating me down to my core. It leaves me weak at the knees and breathless.

His body falls against mine, pressing me deeper into his mattress, as my legs open in invitation for him to take more of me. He grinds his core against mine, and I feel the hardness of his erection, making my heart race and my body ache with need. If he wasn't wearing his jeans and I didn't have on my panties, we'd be connected, flesh against flesh.

My fingers toy with the button of his fly. "You have on too many clothes."

He laughs as I push him onto his back and rip his

jeans and boxers off in one quick pull. They fly over my shoulder behind me as I climb onto his legs and rub my fingers along the sides of his thighs, enjoying the way the rough hairs feel against my fingers. He's all man, and he's mine. I want to please him and do dirty, dirty things to him.

"Is that my shirt?" His fingers toy with the edge of the cotton material.

"It smelled like you."

"Take it off." His voice comes out in a rough growl, and I'm second-guessing, rummaging through his things.

My teeth dig into my bottom lip as my nerves overtake me. "Are you mad I took it?"

"Wildcat, you can wear anything of mine you like, but right now, it's keeping me from touching your beautiful body, and I really need to feel your skin tremble under my fingers." He leans forward and nips at my bottom lip, prying it free from my teeth. His hands trail up my sides, slipping his shirt off over my head and onto the floor somewhere. The cold air shocks my heated flesh, but his fingers pinching on my nipples have all of the air leaving my body. His soft lips suck and bite until my thighs clench. I could come from this alone, but it's not what I'm in the mood for.

"That feels so good, but it's my turn to play."

He chuckles, and the feel of his breath on my nipples has my hips writhing against his hard cock. All laughter stops at that moment as he sucks in a gust of air. "Fuck, you feel good."

"Ax?" My hand slides between us, cupping his balls.

"Yeah?" His fingers dig into my shoulders as I feel his legs tremble.

"I want you in my mouth."

"What my Wildcat wants, she gets." He tucks a strand of hair behind my ear and presses a quick kiss to my lips. When he pulls away and leans back, I slide down his body until I'm eye level with his firm length. I run my nose along the velvety soft skin, satisfying a deep-seated need to smell my man.

My hand fists around his firm flesh, enjoying the way his cock twitches from the sudden touch. I lean forward and suck the head into my mouth. The salty taste explodes on my tongue, only making me crave more. I slide him deeper inside and tighten my lips around the sides of his cock, not stopping until he hits the back of my throat.

"Oh, fuck." He sucks in a gust of air and groans.

I pull away and slide back down a few more times, watching his body tighten from my touch. There's something intoxicating about seeing him fall apart like this. Warmth floods me as my core clenches from every groan I pull from him.

"You're going to be the death of me, Wildcat." He grasps at my hair, holding me in place as he fucks my mouth with hard, violent thrusts. My cheeks hollow out, sucking him in even deeper until he's hitting the back of my throat. The mixture of tobacco and his musky scent spurs me on. A light tap on my shoulder has me stopping. "Slide your legs around and sit on my face. I need to taste you too."

I let him slip from my mouth and do just that. My knees dig into the mattress by his shoulders as I rest my body on top of his. He smacks my butt with his right hand before grabbing a handful. "I've missed this ass, and someday soon I'm going to fuck it."

A mewl of pleasure leaves me the moment I feel the wetness of his tongue slide along my slit. My fingers claw at his thighs, which causes him to let out another groan. His lips wrap around my clit, sucking and toying with it the way he knows I like. Sensation courses through me, turning my body to mush. I'm putty in this man's hands—always have been, always will be.

"Fuck. I could eat you like this for hours." His words leave me breathless, and I'm overcome with the urge to pleasure him. I grab his cock, take him back in my mouth, and continue to work him over. Every lick and suck of his tongue has my body quivering, begging for more. It makes me stroke and work him faster, in tune with the same rhythm he's working me.

My toes curl into the mattress as a fire pools deep in my belly. I let him fall out of my mouth and bury my head against his thigh as my fingers dig into his skin. It's almost too much. "Oh, fuck."

"Give it to me," he demands as he shoves two fingers inside me and curls them. My body trembles from the change in angle. An ache of desire threatens to pull me under. I'm caught up in a euphoric bliss of pleasure and pain. I'm not sure where one ends and the other begins, but I don't care. I lose myself over to the feelings he provokes in me. Pressure builds from deep within my core.

Then he slips a lone finger inside my ass. It's like adding a match to a puddle of gasoline, and I explode. I'm completely filled by him. Every nerve ending is overloaded with sensation. My core clenches as my orgasm overtakes me. Everything inside me convulses until I'm coming all over his face.

He hums in pleasure and continues to wring it out

of me. Wetness spills down my thighs as my heart pounds so fast that it feels like it's going to explode out of my chest. His finger slips out of my ass, and I do my best to come back down from the high he's given me. I've lost all feeling in my face, but Axel isn't done. Not by a long shot.

"Put me back in your mouth. I want us to come together this time." His teeth nibble on my inner thigh as his fingers slip back inside me. He wraps his free arm around my waist, crushing me further against his chest and keeping me in place, as his tongue joins his fingers. They're stretching me, making me feel so full, so complete.

My lips wrap around his length, and I suck him back inside. He's so sensitive that just the slightest bit of tongue has him groaning in appreciation against my pussy. A few more pumps are all it takes to have him twitching and exploding inside my mouth. I swallow every last drop of the salty mixture until he softens before letting him fall out of my mouth and righting myself to slip onto the bed next to him.

Axel wraps an arm around my shoulder, pulling me in deeper against his side, and drops a kiss on the top of my head. We lie there as our heavy breathing mingles into the night air, letting the silence speak louder than any words could.

Something changed tonight. It's been creeping up on us for a while, but it feels like we've come full circle, except for one thing, and I need to come clean about it. There's no need for secrets anymore. I bury my face into his side and gather the strength to confess. Sometimes, it's easier to hide behind the cover of night to unfold my truths.

"I came in here because I had a nightmare."

He pulls me back and stares down at me. "A nightmare about what?"

"The night they took me." The muscles of his abs contract as soon as the words leave my mouth. For a split second, I want to take them back, but that would only stifle any progress we have made to get to this point.

"How long have you been having them?" His thumb strokes light circles against my hip.

"When it first happened, they came every night. I'd wake up in a cold sweat, screaming and terrified they were coming back for me."

"And you never talked to anyone about them because you were hiding." There's no accusation in his voice. Only concern. The hand resting on my hip tightens as he pulls me into a one-arm hug. "I'm so fucking sorry they even got to you in the first place. I won't let anyone hurt you like that ever again, Wildcat."

"I know. As crazy as you drive me, you make me feel safe." I smile against the firm muscles of his chest and inhale our mingled scent.

He tilts my head back to meet his gaze. At the same time, a hand cups the side of my face, bringing me in closer until I feel the warmth of his lips against mine. The kiss is slow and tentative at first, but that all changes the second he enters my mouth. His tongue strokes inside, playing me with a fine precision only he possesses. Tasting myself on his tongue is sexy as hell. If I weren't so spent already, I'd be begging him for another round.

Much too soon he ends it and rests his chin on the side of my head. "You have family at your back, and they will always make sure you're safe. Always." He kisses the top of my head, melting my heart into a puddle. I like the word "family." It's been just my parents and me for so long that it's nice to know I have more.

I close my eyes and fall asleep, feeling something I haven't felt in close to two years—whole.

28

AXEL

The sound of Kelsey's slow, even breathing does little to calm the storm brewing inside of me. I stroke my thumb back and forth along her bare shoulder, trying to block out all thoughts, but it's pointless. My mind keeps falling back to everything that went down with Finn last night. Even the shit sleep I managed to get did nothing to ease the cloud hanging over me.

Last night felt like things had finally shifted for us, and we were getting back to where we should be. All of the shit she's gone through, and this could very well be the thing that pushes her over the edge. The thing that has her walking away from me for good.

I let out a sigh that must be louder than I thought because the next thing I know, Kelsey stirs and is gazing up at me through heavy eyes. Just the sight has all the blood flowing straight to my dick, and everything else fades away.

She rubs the sleep away from her face and smiles. "Hi."

"Hi." I kiss the top of her head and rest my head against hers. Her familiar mango scent fills me with a sense of calm.

She glances toward the window at the sunlight fading away, and her red eyebrows pinch together. "What time is it?"

"Late. Very, very late. I didn't get in until well after four and we didn't actually go to sleep until closer to nine. We slept most of the day." At least she did.

Color fills her cheeks, and I bite back a smile. My Wildcat is hot as fuck when she's acting all shy and shit.

"Oh." She glances up, and I know the moment she takes in my face, and the corners of her blue eyes crease that I can't hide my expressions from her. "Something wrong, Ax?"

For a split second I debate the consequences of keeping this to myself, but fuck it. There's no sense in bullshitting her. "We need to talk about last night."

"Okay." Her whole body tenses up as the light on her face dies and her head drops down to my shoulder, making me feel like a complete asshole.

"Shit. That didn't come out right. This has nothing to do with us. Last night was fucking perfect, and it will happen again and again. On that, you have my word." I pinch the tip of her chin and force her head up until her gaze meets mine. "It's about what happened with Donnelly last night."

"What happened?" Her body relaxes a bit in my arms, but her blue eyes hold so many questions.

I wish there was a better way to deliver bad news, but there isn't. It's best to do it quickly, like a Band-Aid. "He's your uncle."

"What? No way. That's impossible." She presses her plump lips together and shakes her head.

"Believe me, Wildcat. I saw the pictures for myself. It's all true. He's your mom's brother."

My words are met with rapid blinking. She's quiet so long that I almost think she's passed out until she finally speaks. "Are you telling me that my mother was related to the freaking Irish Mob?"

"It appears so."

"Is he the reason my mother's—" Her voice fades, but I know what she's asking.

"No. As far as I can tell, this shit is all on your dad. Whatever relationship Finn and your mom had was kept a secret. They thought it was safer for you that way, but he does have a way of helping us find the bastards that are behind all of this and handling it." I hold her gaze and watch her put the pieces together.

"You're going after them, aren't you?"

"I'm going to make sure that you are safe, and that they will suffer for everything they did to you and your mom." I brace, waiting for a fight, but she surprises me and slams her mouth down against mine in a kiss that has me envisioning her soft lips wrapped around my dick like they were earlier.

She pulls back and rubs the stubble on my cheek, but it's the unshed tears in her eyes that have my pulse racing. "Promise me something."

"Anything."

"Make those fuckers pay. Every last one of them."

"You have my word, Wildcat." My hand slides down the small of her back until I have a handful of her ass. I squeeze the soft flesh and bring her mouth back down to mine for more. There's nothing I want more than to be buried balls deep inside her slick heat. My hand slides around her ass to her pussy, and I waste no time slipping a finger inside her hot, wet heat.

A knock has my finger freezing mid-pump. "We seriously need our own place," I mumble against her mouth and debate on ignoring whoever it is. I'm not dealing with my brothers while suffering a case of blue balls.

"Be nice. It might be important." She smacks my shoulder and laughs, but that quickly turns into a moan as I rub her clit with my thumb.

Another knock comes, and I sigh as I press my forehead to hers. "What?"

"You're needed downstairs." When I don't answer after a beat, Charlee tries again. "Please, Ax?" She never begs me like this unless something is seriously wrong. It can't be Lily because Zane would have woken my ass up. That can mean only one thing.

"Shit."

We jump out of bed and throw our clothes on as fast as we can. I just can't catch a break.

In a matter of minutes, I'm leading Kelsey downstairs as I shove my gun in the waistband of my jeans and walk into what appears to be a complete fucking shit show in the middle of our living room.

Charlee has her arms crossed over her chest, baby monitor in one hand, as she stands next to the doorway to the kitchen and watches my brothers.

Asher has some guy I've never seen before shoved up against a wall, while Zane is having a standoff of his own by the front door with someone else. Both of these fuckers are huge, but I have no clue who they are.

"You fecking hurt my brother, and I'm going to gut

you like a fecking fish," the one in front of Zane threatens. His blue eyes burn into my brother, ready to kill, but Zane doesn't even flinch, and why would he? He could knock him on his ass before he knew what hit him.

"What did I miss?" My head bounces from Zane to Asher, waiting for an answer, and I get one, but it's the one shoved against the wall that gives it.

"My dad sent us." He flashes me a smug grin before shifting his gaze to Kelsey. Then it dawns on me just who I'm dealing with. The features are so similar I'm not sure how I missed it before.

Zane's posture tenses at his words as my jaw clenches. As much as I don't want them here, I need whatever they have.

"Ash, man. Let him talk."

Asher slams him into the wall one more time and gets in his face. "Don't ever come into my house uninvited and threaten my family again or I'll send you back in pieces." He glares at him for another beat before he releases his grip and stalks over to Charlee. His hand cups the back of her head and cradles her against his chest.

Zane shoots me a cold look, but lucky for me it's not directed at me. There's no missing the dark circles under his eyes, and that's an issue Asher and I will tackle another day. I lift my chin his way, and he moves back until he's standing next to me, flanking Kelsey, while the other guy moves to stand next to his brother. We're in another standoff of brothers against brothers.

"You have my word. I won't." The one Asher had against the wall dips his head at Asher and then glances my way and grins.

I cross my arms over my chest and stare him down. He's a cocky bastard, I'll give him that, but there's only enough room for one of us in here, and that's me. "Now that you've all whipped your dicks out to see whose is bigger, would you like to tell me who the hell you are and what the fuck you're doing here?"

"I'm Connor, and that's my brother Rory. Our dad sent us with a gift for you." He holds out a piece of paper to me like it's the winning lottery ticket.

"Is that right? And what makes him think that I'll want any gift he has to offer me?"

His eyes are still fixated on Kelsey as he speaks. If he wasn't her relative, I'd sucker punch him for it. "Trust me, lad. You'll want this one."

I take the piece of paper between my fingers and open it up to find an address. That's it. No name or anything. "What the hell am I supposed to do with this?"

"I guess you'll just have to come with us to find out." Rory shrugs as he takes a long look around our living room.

"He's not going anywhere without us." Asher stands up taller and balls his hands into fists. "But we're not leaving the girls here alone."

"That's what we thought you'd say." Rory laughs as he opens the front door, and in walk the twins from last night, both wearing all black from head to toe, complete with matching black fedoras. The only difference is the one closest to the door has a red feather on the side of his. They might have different tats, but it's too far for me to tell from where I'm standing.

"Howya." The one that's closest to the door tips his hat my way and flashes me a shit-eating grin.

"Who's that fine thing?" The other twin that's near me eyes Charlee, causing Asher to growl.

"Bloody watch it, Keegan." Connor smacks the one wearing the fedora with a red feather upside the head and shakes his head. I have to admit I almost feel bad for him, having had that done to me plenty of times by my own brothers. I don't know how they tell these little shits apart because they're completely identical.

"You lads can have a go, and we'll stay here with your women." Teegan steps further into the room, and that's when I finally see a difference between the two. It's a slight one, but it's enough to keep from mixing them up. He's the most like Finn with his laid-back, watchful persona. That makes Keegan the wild card.

"Like hell I'm leaving my girls here with you." Asher's jaw clenches so hard that I'm surprised he has any teeth left.

"I'm with my brother. It looks like y'all's balls have barely dropped. No way am I trusting you to be able to protect them if something goes wrong."

Keegan laughs in our faces, but it's Teegan that surprises the shit out of me. It happens so fast that I don't have time to realize what's happened until a soft breeze whizzes across my cheek, and a knife goes sailing past my head, embedding into the wall behind me.

Teegan cocks his head to the side and lifts a dark eyebrow in my direction. "You were saying?"

"Fuck." Zane rubs his beard and shakes his head.

Asher doesn't say a word, but the wide-eyed stare he's giving Teegan speaks volumes and mirrors my own thoughts.

"You've got to be shitting me." My head draws back

as I come to terms with what I just saw. It's always the quiet ones.

"That was even faster than last time, Teeg." Keegan punches him in the side of the arm.

"You might say Teegan has a hard-on for knives." Rory lets out a booming laugh and rocks back on the heels of his boots.

"Nice to finally meet you, *mhainséar*." Teegan ignores all of us and lifts the corner of his mouth into a lopsided smile while tipping his hat at Kelsey and then Charlee.

"Uh, hi." Kelsey waves a shaky hand in his direction before she greets the rest of them. Each of them returns a nod of the head, but there's no missing the curiosity burning behind their gazes. I wrap my arm around her and pull her in closer to me, letting them know without words that they may be blood, but she's mine, and I don't give a fuck if they like it or not.

"You ready now? Or are you needing more proof of what us Donnelly boys can do?" Connor crosses his arms over his chest and stares us down.

"I mean, it was *okay*." I clear my throat a couple of times and shrug my shoulders. No way am I going to admit to him how badass that was.

"We'll be waiting outside." Connor motions for Rory to head out the door, but before he can make it far, I stop him.

"Now, hold on a minute. Why are y'all the ones driving?" My eyebrows pinch together.

"If you want to take your truck, be my guest." Connor shrugs.

"What the fuck do you know about Willie Mae?"

The edges of Connor's mouth curl into a smile as he

and Rory exit out the front door, leaving me to stew on their words.

"Y'all put them up to this?" I shoot my brothers a look and, in return, get two headshakes. With no other choice, I kiss Kelsey on the top of the head and storm out after them.

Looks like us Savage brothers are about to go hunting with the Donnelly brothers. God help anyone who gets in our way.

29

AXEL

It took us over two hours of stiff conversation to drive to the address that Finn provided. The sun's gone down, and now I'm trapped inside a blacked-out van watching a modern two-story home in suburban hell between my two tense-as-fuck brothers. Lucky for us, it's a rare cloudless night in Georgia, and the moon is bright as shit. Doesn't calm my agitation one bit, though. I prefer the wide-open spaces of the country. Being this far in the city is making my skin itch with pent-up anxiety.

Asher spent the entire drive glaring at the back of Connor's and Rory's heads, waiting to strike if necessary. I'm not sure what they were thinking by putting us in the seats behind them. In doing so, it's made them ripe for the picking. It could be a show of trust, or it could be a way to lure us into a false sense of security right before they gut us and dump our asses on the side of the road. Time will tell, I guess.

Zane hasn't said a word since we left either, but unlike Asher, his silence is the most concerning. He's like a ticking bomb, and I just hope we're not trapped in this van when he finally explodes.

I take another hit off my cigarette and shift against the tan leather seat once more. What we're waiting for, I have no fucking clue.

"Problem, lad?" Rory speaks up from the passenger seat. Despite our brief interactions, I can't get an accurate read on him or Connor. The twins and Kennedy I've figured out after a few seconds, but these two remain enigmas. A fact that bugs the shit out of me to no end.

My head lifts up to meet Connor's gaze in the rearview mirror head-on. The cherry of his cigarette casts a slight glow on his face, but other than that, it's blank. There are no emotions whatsoever. Any chance I've had of gauging him is shot to shit. He keeps his stuff locked down as tight as Asher. "I don't like being left in the dark. Don't take me for a dumb country boy. Y'all know more than you're telling me."

"Maybe. Maybe not." Rory twists around and looks down his nose at me. "Guess you'll just have to wait and see, won't you, Country."

The snarky edge in his voice has my fists clenching. I'd love nothing more than to knock this cocky fuck down a peg or two, but since we're in a confined space, I hold myself back and grit my teeth. Asher, on the other hand, gives no fucks about confined spaces. The only good thing to come out of him being locked up for six years. He leans forward, ready to launch himself over me to beat Rory's ass, but before he can, I slam my arm across his chest and give him a slight shake of my head. That small movement is enough to keep him in his seat but won't hold him for long. At least Zane is too zoned out to flip his shit. I'm not sure I could keep both of them under control.

"Guess you have to have big brother fight your battles for you." Rory flicks the tip of his cigarette in my direction. I lift my fist, ready to beat his ass, but Connor gets there before me. He slaps Rory upside the head with an open hand.

"What the feck, Con?" Rory rubs at the spot that his brother just smacked.

"Shut the feck up, Ror. Or I'll kick your stupid arse myself."

I laugh at the glare on his face.

"What?" Rory snaps.

"I've been wanting to do that all damn night."

"Feck right off, you." Rory shakes his head.

A door slams open, putting an end to our issues, and we see movement.

My pulse pounds in my ears as I get a good look at the bald figure that's strolling over toward a blue sedan. "Carrick."

"You sure, Ax?" Asher asks, but never takes his eyes off the prize.

"I'd never forget the prick that blew up Willie Mae and shot at us." My eyes narrow at him and then flick back over to where Carrick is. Stupid fuck is walking around like he has no cares in the world. Little does he know that that's about to change. "Are we going to grab him or what?"

"Patience, lad. There are too many eyes on us here. We know where he's going, and we'll snatch him then." Connor exhales a cloud of smoke and tilts his head.

"Bullshit. I want to take him now." I slide toward the van door, but Zane doesn't budge. My foot kicks his shin to snap him out of whatever dark thoughts he's been battling to gain his attention and prepare for the retaliatory punch, but he doesn't even blink.

"He's right, Ax. We need to be smart about this. There's no telling what connections he has. They get wind that it was us, and we're fucked." He plays with the mess of hair on his head.

"Oh, sure. Come back to the land of the living to take their side. Thanks a lot, asshat." I shake my head and let what they're saying sink in. A part of me wants to jump out of the van and grab him, but they all have a damn point. I need to think with my head and not be impulsive for once. This is why, instead of jumping over Zane, we watch him slip inside his car and pull away.

Connor cranks the ignition, and the van crawls in the direction of Carrick's taillights. He follows at a decent distance behind him so that he's never out of our sight for long. I'm pretty sure he's done this a time or twenty, given their family's line of work.

All the way through the dark downtown streets to a section of abandoned warehouses, I hold my breath. My fingers twitch from the excitement of the hunt, like they always do before we capture our target.

"You're going too slow. Use your fecking gas pedal or you're going to lose him, Con." Rory taps his hand on the dashboard like that's going to somehow make Connor pick up speed.

"Feck off. I'm doing fine. Any closer and he'll see us, you fecking idiot."

My heart races the longer I watch his taillights. We're so close I can feel his blood on my hands. He pulls through a rusted-out chain-link fence all the way around back, away from the streetlights. Connor follows through the fence, but instead of turning right, he makes a sharp left that pulls us around to the opposite side and gives us an unobstructed view. The moon gives us just enough light to see what's happening.

Carrick pulls up next to a black Jeep and kills his engine. He and his new guest exit their vehicles and lean against them.

While they're distracted with conversation, we slip out of the van and creep along the building until we're close enough to hear their mumbled voices.

"Like lambs to slaughter." Rory stabs the butt of his cigarette against the metal of the building and cocks his gun as he flashes me a wide-toothed grin. "You lads ready to play?"

Neither Connor nor Asher speaks, but their eyes are focused on our targets. I glance at Zane, and he's already locked his shit down, ready to do what we do best—fuck shit up.

30

AXEL

"**J**esus, how much do these feckers weigh?" Rory groans as both he and I carry an unconscious Carrick to a wooden chair that's sitting in the center of an abandoned warehouse on the other side of town that they "use."

"Stop your bitching. You got the lighter fella," Connor grunts while he, Asher, and Zane bring in the other guy we found him with.

"Feck off." Rory shakes his head as we prop him down into a seated position. My brothers and Connor strap the other guy down to a metal table, but I don't give much thought to what else they've got planned because I have my own shit to handle.

"Here." Zane tosses us some rope from the bag he brought in, and I get to work binding his wrists to the arms of the chair, while Rory does the same to his legs.

Once I'm sure he's secure and not going anywhere, I stand back and look for my toy of choice. My gaze travels along the walls, and there are nothing but options. This room is like a serial killer's wet dream.

Anything I can think of to torture the truth out of him is at my disposal.

"What'll it be, Ax?" Asher hangs back, letting me know without words that I'm running the show with whatever device of my choosing. A glisten of metal catches my attention, and a smile spreads across my face as I pick up the hammer and box of nails from the shelf.

"Interesting choice." Asher's dark eyebrows raise as he eyes my hands, but the corner of his mouth twitches.

"It's not my bat, but it'll do." I hang the hammer over my shoulder and make to move toward Carrick, but I'm stopped short by Rory. He's a few cans shy of a six-pack.

He pinches his cigarette between his lips and messes with his phone, hooking it up to a playing dock, until "Beautiful Day" by U2 blares through the room. "That's better."

"Seriously?" I cock an eyebrow at him as I study his face. I'm not sure if he's fucking with me or not.

"What? They're talented Irish bastards." He shrugs and flashes me a wide smirk that says the engine is running but there's no one behind the wheel.

"Whatever, man." I shake my head as he inhales a deep breath, closes his eyes, and tilts his head back. I wait for him to move, but he doesn't. It's like he's lost in a trance.

"What the fuck is he doing?" Asher puffs out his chest next to me, no doubt getting ready to blow his top at this. Unless it's for his girls, he has the patience of a gnat.

We like to get in, fuck shit up, and get out without making a sound. Not the Donnelly boys. They're as stealthy as dropping a bomb in a damn library.

"Is he meditating?" Zane cranes his head to the side and strokes the tip of his beard, looking as lost as the rest of us at Rory's behavior.

"It helps him." Connor shrugs as we continue to watch his brother do whatever the fuck it is he's doing.

A few more beats pass by before Rory finally opens his eyes, and there's no missing the dark glaze that's taken over. He cracks his neck from side to side like a boxer and shakes out his hands as he bounces on his feet. "It feels like Thanksgiving. Let's carve up this fecking turkey." He pulls a knife out of the waistband of his jeans as he and Connor retreat to their side of the room to do their thing.

My brothers and I stalk over to where Carrick is strapped to the chair. I slap his cheek, but he doesn't even stir. "Damn. Fucker's out cold."

"Not for long." Asher tosses a bucket of water on Sleeping Beauty, and judging by the way he jerks his head up, it must be cold as fuck. His blue eyes burn into mine as he takes slow, shallow breaths. I'm going to enjoy watching this fucker break.

"You?" His dark eyebrows pull together as he lets out a hollow laugh. That only fuels my fire.

Whistling to myself, I take out a nail from the box and then turn my glare back on Carrick.

"How original." Carrick shakes his head at me, but there's no missing the bead of sweat glistening against the bald skin of his head.

Without warning, I smack him upside the head with my fist. "That's for Willie Mae."

"Who?" His eyes narrow at me as blood drips down his chin.

"My truck, you stupid fuck." When I'm met with

silence, I bring the hammer down on his hand without warning. He squeals like the pussy he is and it feeds my soul, but it's not enough.

I nod with my chin at Asher and Zane. They know exactly what I'm asking without words. We've perfected this move like a well-timed song and dance. Zane stands behind Carrick, while Asher puts his hands on the bald prick's shoulders, giving them a good squeeze.

"Feck ye! Ye fecking pussy!" Carrick struggles against Asher's hold, but it's pointless. He ain't going anywhere. Asher has a death grip on him.

I press the tip of the nail against his smashed hand and place the head of the hammer on top before looking him in the eye. "You know why you're here. So, save us all some time and just tell me what I want to know."

"I'm not telling ye shit." Carrick's nostrils flare as a vein on the side of his head pulses.

I bring the hammer down so fast that he has no time to tense up. The nail drives right through his hand and embeds into the wood of the chair. Bono's voice drowns out his screams as blood drips down onto the dirty floor and I can almost see why Rory digs this shit. It's kind of cathartic. I place another nail on top of his other hand and smile. "Let's try that again. Shall we?"

"I have nothing to tell ye." He pants through the pain, and I'm almost sure he's close to passing out. It takes a couple of tries for him to get his words out. For some reason, his stubbornness is pissing me off more than normal. Sweat drips down my back as I grind my teeth so hard my jaw aches. Time to try a different approach.

"You ever play the game Whack-a-Mole, Carrie?" I

swing the hammer around by the handle in rhythm with the music as Bono belts out the chorus, and I watch my words penetrate through his thick head. "You don't mind if I call you Carrie, do you?" Not that I give a fuck if he does.

"Go to hell," he groans as blood drips down his neck.

Without warning, I bring the hammer down on the chair right between his legs. "Oops. Looks like I missed. Your dick must be pretty small for my aim to be such shit."

"Ye're fecking crazy!" Carrick jerks against the chair in a piss-poor attempt to avoid being hit with the hammer.

"You have no idea." I swing the wooden handle around and watch him squirm. "Tell me who hired you. Or the next time I might actually hammer your tiny dick to this chair."

"Feck ye!" Carrick spits out between a mouthful of blood.

"Sorry. Wrong answer." With a smile plastered on my face, I slam the hammer down between his legs so hard the wood splits, and this time, I don't miss. It slams down right on his dick. He lets out a blood-curdling scream that would make any grown man cry. Even Asher and Zane wince from where they're standing. I have to admit it does make my own dick hurt, but it's nothing less than he deserves.

I take a deep drag of the cigarette Zane handed me earlier as I crane my neck to the side, watching Carrick try to curl in on himself. His face turns a bright shade of green. "That looks like it hurts."

The guy that Rory and Connor are carving up

shouts at that moment, causing Carrick to lift his head in his direction. My fingers splay over the top of his bald head and twist his face back to me. I'm sure watching them carve his friend up is fucking with his head, but I still need his complete attention. "Don't worry about him. They'll be done with him soon enough." His pupils are dilated as his eyes glaze over. He's seconds from passing out, and I can't let that happen. I snap in his face a couple of times to bring his attention back where it needs to be, but he doesn't even flinch. "Focus, Carrie."

"I can't. He'll fecking kill me." His chin rests on his chest as his head bobbles and blood dribbles down the side of his face onto his neck. The fucker is starting to sound like a broken record.

"What the fuck do you think we're going to do?" Asher digs his fingers deeper into Carrick's shoulders, driving his point home.

"My brother's right." I shove the tip of the hammer against his chest. "You will die for your sins. Only choice left for you is how badly do you want to suffer first? You tell us what we want to know, I'll end it quickly, but you jerk me around, and I'll move onto your balls next."

A few beats of silence tick by as he glares at me. Then his lips break out into a wide smirk. "Ye really think ye have it all figured out don't ye? That we'd make it that easy for ye?" He takes one look at my face and shakes his head as he lets out a maniacal laugh. "I didn't think ye were that bloody stupid, but he was right. Ye fecking fell for it."

"Fell for what?" My eyes narrow at him as I do my best to keep my temper under control.

"Loren knew ye were sweet on her even before ye

came lookin'. Knew he could lure ye in to bring her back for us."

"You're lying." A lead weight settles in my gut at his words, and I swallow the lump forming in my throat.

"Ye made it too feckin' easy. Her pussy must be feckin' gold. I can't wait to have a taste of it for meself." He's talking, but I'm not hearing anything else he's saying. My head's too busy spinning at that one revelation. We've been fucking played.

Blood pounds in my ears as his words settle deep into my bones. My knuckles whiten against the handle of the hammer as my brain struggles to make sense of it. Everything comes roaring back to me in a flood, and I'm all out of patience with this asshole. He's wasting my time. Time that could be spent with Kelsey. I drop the hammer and pull out my Glock, burying the barrel against his temple, and pull the trigger.

I can't breathe. My chest is constricting in on itself as the warmth of his blood and bits of what I'm sure is his brain matter coat my face. I shoot my eyes over to Asher and Zane. Both of them come to the same conclusion I do. "Her fucking dad set us up."

Asher pulls out his phone, and his face goes ashen. "Fuck!"

"What's wrong?" I shove my gun back into the waistband of my jeans and keep my focus on my brother.

"Cameras picked up cars circling the house." Asher's looking at his phone as a muscle jerks in his cheek.

"Shit!" I'm seconds from running out the door when Rory's voice stops me.

"Problem?" He's covered in blood and resembles something out of a horror movie, not that I don't look much better with the blood and brain matter all over me.

"We need to get the fuck out of here. They're at my house." Asher's halfway to the door when he stops and glances at the two dead bodies we've left in our wake. "What about them?"

"Leave them." Rory grabs his phone from the dock, bathing us in silence. "My dad has cleaners that'll take care of it for us. We have to move now."

The five of us rush to the van and tear out of the parking lot as fast as we can. Rory drives this time while Connor pulls out his phone and makes a call. Asher and I do the same, but ours keep going to voicemail.

"Teeg, get the feck out of there now. You hear me." A muffled voice echoes through the phone before Connor speaks again. "It's a setup. The whole thing was a diversion to get us out of the way. Take them to Dad's house, and we'll meet you there."

My blood runs cold as his words hit me. We played right into their fucking hands. And Kelsey's going to pay the price.

31
KELSEY

From the time the guys walked out the front door, there's been an awkwardness lingering in the room. One I'm having a hard time moving past. Even when Lily woke up from her nap a few hours ago and Keegan helped Charlee bring her back out here, I've been feeling off. I can't explain the heavy feeling in the pit of my stomach, but I suck in a deep breath and attempt to exhale it all out. My fingers twist in my lap as I attempt to slow my racing pulse, but it's pointless. I won't be able to calm down until Axel and the guys are back here safe and sound.

Keegan slumps back against the couch with his ankle resting on the knee of his other leg, looking at home with Lily nestled in the crook of his arm. Tattoos run along one of his arms and both hands. My eyes trail up the intricate pieces of art, admiring them. I'm sure Asher would shit himself if he saw his daughter content with him. Then again, maybe it's all his tattoos that are soothing her.

He catches me staring and smiles. "You stare at all your cousins like that? Or am I just that bad-arse?"

"No, it's always been just me and my parents. I'm an only child, and we don't have much family." I squirm in my seat, unsure why hearing my life explained out loud sounds so depressing.

"You do now, *mhainséar.*" Teegan smiles from his spot on the sofa. Feels weird to hear him say that, but also comforting at the same time.

"Does that mean 'cousin'?" I tilt my head to the side and study Teegan. He resembles Keegan, but there are slight differences to me. His nose turns up a bit more at the tip, and he doesn't have as many tattoos on his arm as his brother. Not to mention he seems the more serious one of the two.

"It does." Teegan lifts the corner of his mouth into a slight smile.

"The better looking ones, anyway." Keegan nudges Teegan's shoulder as he lets out a laugh that lights up his face, showing how young he really is.

"No doubt about that." Teegan slaps his shoulder and peers down at Lily as she makes a noise. "I don't know why she likes your ugly face so much."

"Feck off. She has good taste, is all." Keegan hands a drooling Lily his fedora and lets her chew on the ends of it. "She's a cute lil' thing." He runs a tattooed finger along her chubby cheeks, his fair skin a deep contrast to her olive one. The shamrock tattoo on his finger catches my eye. It's done in a similar design to the butterfly my mother had on her wrist.

"See something you like?" Keegan's laugh breaks my stare as I flick my gaze up to him.

"Your tattoo. My mother had a butterfly one on her wrist that was similar in style to it."

"It's a Celtic design." The corners of his blue eyes crease as he pins me in place with an assessing look.

"I'm sorry about your mum. We didn't know her, but our dad told us all about how close they were." Teegan offers me a small smile.

"Thanks." A dull ache pings in my chest at his words. With everything going on, I haven't had the proper time to mourn her loss, and it kills me.

Our conversation stalls out until Keegan breaks it. His nose wrinkles as he sniffs the air a few times and then pulls his shirt over his nose. "Oh, bloody hell. I think the little one has nasty arse juice."

"I'll take her." Charlee laughs from her spot in the corner. I've been so absorbed in these two that I forgot she was even here until now. She takes Lily from Keegan and smells her butt. "Yup, that's a bad one." She plants a kiss on Lily's cheek and goes into the other room to change her.

The second Charlee rounds the corner out of sight, a phone rings. Teegan pulls it out of his pocket and answers.

"Yeah?" A beat of silence goes by as the voice on the other end fires off at a rapid pace into the phone. "Stall the ball for a minute, Connor. I can't understand you." Teegan toys with the edge of his fedora as Keegan sits up straighter at the mention of their brother's name. The tension in the room has multiplied tenfold. His eyes flick toward mine as he continues to listen to his brother. "Yeah, she's right here. All the women are fine." His dark eyebrows pinch together, but he doesn't break my stare. "Shit. Let me see your phone, Keeg."

Keegan hands him his phone without complaint, and we watch as Teegan pulls something up. Whatever he sees as a muscle in his jaw jerking.

"What the bloody hell do you want us to do? Are you sure that's smart? We might have a better chance if we stay and—" Teegan listens a beat longer, leaving us to wait on pins and needles.

I hold my breath waiting as I slide to the edge of my seat and watch Teegan for any signs of distress, but he has one hell of a poker face for someone so young.

"Got it." He hangs up the phone and turns to his brother. "Tell Charlee to pack up anything she needs for the baby as fast as she can, we need to leave."

Keegan nods and goes into the other room without a word.

My muscles tense at the clipped edge to his tone. "What's wrong? Why do we need to leave?"

"I know you don't know us that well, but I need you to trust me. They asked us to get you out of here and to my dad's, so that's what we're going to do." He glances down to my bare feet. "You have some shoes you can slip on fast?"

"Yeah, I do." I jump up from my spot on the loveseat and run upstairs into my room. I grab my tan cowgirl boots and slide them on in record time before I rush back down the stairs to find Teegan waiting by the door. Keegan is next to him with a diaper bag strapped to his chest, and a distraught Charlee is standing between the two of them, carrying a squirming Lily in her arms.

"You take Charlee and the little one in her car. I'll take Kelsey with me in our truck." Teegan pulls out a gun and cocks the trigger as he issues orders.

"Why are we splitting up?" I can't stop the shaking

in my voice, and judging by the look Teegan gives me, he picked up on it as well.

"We have about five minutes before they bust through the gate and all hell breaks loose. It's safer for Lily if we take two cars and lead them away from her."

"Keys?" Keegan holds his hand out in Charlee's direction.

"In the diaper bag." She points with her chin to the bag before squeezing me in a one-armed hug. "Love you, Kels, and be careful."

"Yeah, love you too. We'll see you at the house." Lily squirms between us, and I drop a kiss to the top of her soft dark hair, inhaling her clean scent as if it's for the last time, and I hope like hell it's not.

With my heart in my throat, I watch my best friend walk out the door with Keegan. Teegan squeezes my shoulder and nudges me along outside to his truck.

"Get in the front seat and stay down."

I do as he says without complaint as he climbs into the driver's side. Without a word, he turns the ignition, and we drive around the side of the house to what I'm guessing is the back way off of the property.

We make it a quarter of the way down the back road when a pair of headlights glare right behind us. I hold my breath and hope, like hell, that they're just a regular car passing by. Several beats of tense silence go by as we wait.

"Teegan?" My palms sweat the closer they get to us.

"I see them." His eyes do a quick glance in the mirror and then back to the road. He slams down on the gas, but they stay glued to us. The vein in my neck jumps the longer they keep with us. Then we're hit from behind, and my body jerks forward so hard that my neck cracks. "Fecking bastards." His grip tightens on the steering wheel as he locks out his arms. A loud pop echoes behind us right before the glass of the back window shatters. I protect my head with my hands as more bullets rain down on us. "Scoot down low in your seat, Kelsey," Teegan orders as he scans the road ahead, hopefully finding us a way out of this. Out of nowhere, another set of headlights flashes in our eyes as they come at us head-on.

"We're going to crash," I scream as Teegan swerves to the side to avoid them, but we're pushed from behind at the same time, causing our truck to spin and flip over.

"Brace yerself."

That's the last thing I hear before the sound of metal twisting hits my ears and the world goes black.

32
AXEL

I'm on the edge of my seat the whole way back with my heart in my throat. Nothing inside of me will settle down until we reach the house. Asher is just as tense next to me, and I can feel every emotion radiating off of him in waves. I keep replaying everything over in my head, wondering how I could have missed the signs. The truth is I let my emotions do the talking instead of paying better attention. If something happens to Charlee or Wildflower because of my oversight, I'll never forgive myself.

When we pull through the security gate and bypass the cluster of guys with guns into Finn's driveway, I see Charlie's car, and a piece of my heart settles. It still won't be complete until I have Kelsey in my arms.

Asher doesn't wait until Rory kills the engine before he's out and rushing inside the house. The rest of us follow right after him to find the living room packed full of Donnellys.

Finn's sitting on a cream sofa with a cigar in one hand, and his other arm is wrapped around Kennedy.

Keegan is sitting on the love seat across from her, toying with his fedora.

The muscles in my body begin to relax as I watch Asher wrap his girls in his arms. They're here. They're safe. I glance around, searching for that familiar fleck of red hair, but when I come up empty, an uneasy feeling creeps over me. "Where's Kelsey?"

"They never made it here." Tears pool in Charlee's green eyes as she shakes her head. "They were supposed to be right behind us. We should never have split up." She bursts into sobs and buries her face in Asher's chest. He kisses the top of her head, but there's no mistaking the clench of his jaw as a lead weight settles in my gut. This can't be happening.

"Where's Teegan?" Rory glances around the room, just now realizing that we are one twin short.

Connor is standing next to him wearing the same grim expression we all are.

"He was bringing Kelsey in our truck. We separated to divert their attention and keep them from harming the baby, but Charlee's right. We should never have separated." Keegan swallows down the rest of his words as he runs a hand through his dark hair.

"Nonsense, Keeg. It's not your fault." Kennedy sniffles, and Finn squeezes her tighter against his side. I sense Zane tense next to me at the sight, but I have my own shit to deal with at the moment.

"Ye did exactly what I taught ye to do." Finn holds Keegan's stare. Their conversation sounds like it's happening in a tunnel as my heart pounds against my chest so hard I feel like it's going to crack in two.

"Son of a bitch!" I kick over a nearby table, causing the glass top and all of its contents to shatter against the marble floor. Lily jumps into Charlee's arms as her little fists wave around in the air. Her soft cries have me feeling like the biggest dick on the planet. "Sorry, Wildflower."

Charlee pats her tiny back and shushes her as Asher escorts them both into the other room, but not before he shoots me a look that clearly warns me he'll have my balls if I ever do something like that again.

Nobody says a word for what seems like hours until Finn breaks it. He glances at me and Rory and shakes his head. "Ye two are a feckin' mess. Did I teach ye nothin'? Shower and meet me in my office in ten." I open my mouth to argue, but he gets there first. "Ken will show ye where ye can clean up." With that, he pushes up to a standing position and exits the room, leaving me with my heart in my throat.

Kennedy pushes her glasses further up her pert nose and motions for me to follow her. "This way."

I trail behind her, up the stairs, and into one of the bedrooms that leads to a massive suite of a bathroom. In a fog, I step through the threshold and into the huge space.

"For what it's worth, my dad will find them both." She stops in the doorway and peers up at me through her glasses, revealing deep blue eyes. Up until now, it's escaped my attention how similar her features are to Kelsey, and that only twists the knife in my gut deeper.

My mind is spinning in a million different directions, and the only response I can manage is a small nod.

Her hands clasp in front of her as she pastes a smile on her face and watches me for a second. "The towels are in that cupboard right there, and fresh clothes are in the cupboard next to that one." When I don't say anything, she rocks back on the heels of her feet and clears her throat a couple of times. I should probably say something so I don't come off as such a dick to Kelsey's cousin, but words aren't coming to me. "I'll leave you to it then." She spins and leaves me alone, but not before I catch a glimpse of Zane's back as he follows after her like a stalker. I'm not even touching that. I have enough issues of my own to deal with at the moment without adding his on top of it.

I step further into the marble bathroom and up to the sink, wondering how everything got so fucked up so fast. My nostrils flare as I stare back at my bloody reflection and try to rein in my breathing, but it's pointless. Everything hits me all at once. All the shit they've done. All the shit I've handed to them on a silver fucking platter. It's like my heart has been ripped out of my chest. I can't stand to look at myself right now. My hand curls into a fist and slams down against the mirror, shattering the glass. Blood coats my knuckles, but I don't feel a thing. Nothing registers except two things. They took her from me, and it's all my fault.

"We'll find you." It's a promise—one I won't break. I'll burn the whole damn world down to keep it if I have to. Or else I'm going to burn the world down to keep it.

33
KELSEY

My tongue sticks to the roof of my mouth as I come to. A throbbing pain radiates from the side of my head and quickly spreads to the rest of my body, but I swallow down the discomfort and ignore the fact that my throat feels like sandpaper. It takes a couple of tries before I'm able to blink the fog from my eyes. When I do, I'm greeted with a water-stained tile ceiling glaring back at me. I shift to sit up, taking note of the softness of a mattress dipping underneath my weight and touching my bare feet. When I glance down at my appearance, my eyebrows scrunch together. Someone has taken off my boots but had the decency to leave me fully dressed.

Moonlight shines in from a tiny window above me, illuminating my surroundings. Judging by the height and the block walls, I'm guessing I'm in somebody's basement.

After a couple of failed attempts, I manage to sit up, and a wave of nausea hits me so fast that the entire room spins. All of my blood rushes to my legs, leaving black spots clouding my vision. I cup the side of my head to keep from passing out. It helps to ease some of the sharpness that pounds against my temple, but the flesh is so tender I wince. Dried blood coats my hand when I pull away, causing an onslaught of images to flash before my eyes. A car, Teegan shouting, the sound of twisting metal before everything went black. It's all coming back to me in a flood. My limbs shake from the memories. I need to get out of here.

It takes a few more seconds for me to fully gain my bearings. I glance around the small space and find nothing but a door and block walls staring back at me. My memory is still a bit fuzzy, but I'm coherent enough to know I need to find a way out of here. I stumble to my bare feet, wincing when the cold cement floor seeps into my bones. On shaky limbs, I attempt to walk toward the nearest wall.

"Ye're awake." My body jumps at the sound of that voice. Something about it is vaguely familiar, but in my current state, I can't place it.

I spin around toward the doorway, and my heart damn near jumps out of my chest. My eyes make their way up from his penny loafers, stopping dead on that puka shell necklace. All the blood drains from my face. "Alan?"

He steps further into the room until he's right in front of me. The second his brown eyes meet mine, I want to scream. "Hello, Lorelei." He cocks his head to the side and flashes me a blinding smile. "Or should I say Kelsey?"

"What? How?" My eyes narrow as I struggle to make sense of what the hell is happening right now. It knocks my balance out of whack, and I have to lean against the block wall before I face plant into the floor. "Where's Teegan?"

He lifts a finger to brush a stray strand of hair out of my face as he looks down at me. "He's the least of yer worries right now. Ye should be worried about what I'm going to do to ye."

"Where. Is. He?" I smack his hand away and slink further against the block wall, hoping it'll swallow me up whole.

"I've been watchin' ye a long time." He ignores me and keeps talking. "I had to make sure yer da stayed in line, and what better way to do that than to hold over him the one thing he loves most? His daughter."

"Alan—" I attempt to plead with him, but he cuts me off.

"Murphy." He strokes the side of my face, taking in my appearance. "Call me by me name." He leans in so close that I can feel his lips brush against mine. His fingers trail up and down the side of my neck, slipping lower each time. When I don't respond fast enough, he fists a hand in my hair and squeezes until my scalp burns. "Say it!"

Everything inside me shrivels at his cold touch. I struggle to keep my breathing steady. If I'm going to get myself out of here, I need to keep calm. Timing is everything. I'll play along for now. "Murphy." His name feels like acid on my tongue the second it tumbles past my lips.

"Good girl." A hungry gaze burns behind his eyes as he follows the line of his fingers brushing past my shoulder, stopping on my breast. He palms it, kneading my soft flesh. The tips of his fingers pinch my nipple so hard I yelp, and it only seems to excite him further. "Ye like it rough? Don't ye?"

I take advantage of his distraction and knee him right in the balls. It's enough that his hand falls away from my body, and I'm able to run for the open door, but I don't make it even a couple of steps before he grabs me by the hair and slams me back against the wall.

"Ye feckin' cunt." The hand gripping my hair clamps down even tighter, and I lose it. I claw and kick at him with everything I have, but it's no use. He's too strong. "Enough." The hand fisting my hair slams my head back against the wall so hard I see stars. "Where is it?" Every muscle in his body is rigid as his heavy breathing fills my ears.

"I don't know what you're talking about."

"Don't lie to me, ye stupid cunt." Without warning, he backhands me with his free hand. Fire erupts along the same side of my face that's been throbbing since I woke up. The wet warmth of blood drips down my bottom lip as his cold eyes glare down at me. Those two black orbs send a shiver straight through me. They'll suck out my soul and spit it back out if I let him. "I know ye have the SD card."

I cup the side of my face and fight the urge to vomit. An explosion of pain is overtaking me. "I don't know anything about an SD card."

"Bullshit." His fingers pull on my hair, forcing my head back past the point of comfort. He leans in so close that I gag on the stale stench of his breath. "I know ye have it. Tell me where the feck it is, right now. Or yer in for a rough night."

"I'm not lying to you, I swear." My cheek burns from

his hit, but I refuse to cower down to him. I straighten my shoulders and get into his face. "I have no clue what you're talking about, and even if I did, I wouldn't tell you jack shit, asshole."

He lets out a hollow laugh that have the little hairs on the back of my neck stand on end. "Looks like ye might need a little motivation." His neck cranes in the direction of the open doorway. "Bring him in."

A huge guy who has burns covering the whole left side of his face comes in, but it's who he throws onto the floor of the room that takes my breath away.

"Dad?"

34
AXEL

While cleaning up in the shower, I replayed everything over in my head, and I'm not happy with what I've figured out. There's more than one player with a piece on the chessboard, which is why I barrel into Finn's office and head straight for the Irish bastard himself. Before I can get anywhere near him, my brothers are on me, holding me back from breaking his jaw.

"What the fuck, Ax?" Zane grunts from under the weight of my struggle, but neither he nor Asher releases me.

"Get your shit together, now!" Asher shoves me so hard that I stumble out of their hold and back a few steps.

"This motherfucker played us." I point a finger in Finn's direction and attempt to calm my breathing.

Rory and Connor step in front of us, arms crossed against their chests like they're his fucking bodyguards, but it doesn't cause the red filling my vision to cease any. I bounce back on my feet and attempt to run through them, but Zane slams a hand against my chest. He narrows his eyes at my words, but it's Asher's reaction that has me on edge.

"You knew?"

"No, but after we got back here and I thought about everything, shit was starting to connect." Asher turns around and crosses his arms over his chest, like Rory and Connor, daring them to try and fuck with us. "And I'm not happy with what I've figured out."

"For feck's sake. She was never in any danger." A muscle twitches in my jaw as Finn breaks our stare down.

"Bullshit." I stab my finger in his direction. "If that was Kennedy, you'd have my nuts in a vise for even thinking of doing what you did."

Zane tenses up next to me at the mention of her name, and I almost feel bad for digging the knife deeper into his open wound—almost.

A flicker of darkness creeps across Finn's face at the mention of his daughter, but his gaze never wavers from mine. It happened so fast that if I blinked, I would have missed it, but it was there plain as day. I've struck a nerve, and I plan on hitting more than that if he doesn't give me the answers I want. Answers I deserve.

"That's enough, lad." Finn's sitting calmly in his chair, but I can see the storm brewing in his eyes. "Sit yer arse down, and I'll explain it all to ye." He gestures with his hand for Rory and Connor to take a seat on the couch next to Keegan. Unease fills me when Keegan averts his eyes and won't meet my stare. Something is off, and I don't like that he knows and the rest of us are left in the dark.

I take advantage of the space I've been given, stepping closer until his desk is mere inches from me. My hands press down on top of the papers that litter it, and I have his full attention. Without turning around, I can feel the heat of Zane and Asher flanking me on either side. "Start talking."

Finn takes a puff on his cigar, tilting his head to the side as he lets out a cloud of smoke, not the least bit threatened by me. "It's amazin' how much information these wee cards can hold." He toys with a tiny black square between his fingers as he holds my attention.

"So what?" My eyebrows pinch together as I continue to study him. I'm not sure where he's going with this, but he better get to the fucking point real quick.

"I told ye I never stopped watchin' over her. That includes her da. Always told me sister he was a gobshite, that one. He thought he could play a man's game, but he wasn't smart enough to remember the first rule. Never feck with me family."

"Kelsey is *my* family. Not yours." The corded muscles in my neck tense from the strain of keeping my shit together.

The corner of his mouth lifts into a half smile, but other than that he doesn't acknowledge that I've even spoken a word. "Her da thought he was smarter than everyone else, untouchable because of who he is. That's how the stupid feck got in over his head and ended up owing a shite load of money to the wrong people."

"What does any of this have to do with Kelsey?" My eyes dart between his, ready to jump across the desk and slam my fist into his throat if he doesn't hurry up and get to the fucking point.

"Everythin'. This wee thing is what they've been

after this whole time, and the fecker had her hide for him."

He reaches down and pulls out several pictures of Kelsey. There are several of her going and coming from Gilley's. Some are even as far back as two years ago, when she first left Georgia and made it to California.

"See anythin' interestin' in these?" Finn cocks his head to the side and waits me out.

I study each image, looking for anything that sticks out, but I come up empty. "All I see is two years of stalking your niece. You fucking psycho."

Finn ignores my dig and keeps pushing his point home. "Take another look. What's she wearin' in every single photograph?"

Things click into place as soon as he speaks, and I feel like a dumbass for not putting it together sooner. "Her fucking boots."

"Aye. The bastard hid all of his files in something he knew she'd never lose—the sole of one of her boots. That's why he was more than happy to help her disappear."

"I sent me older boys over to help ye sort out the feckers that shot at her and the other two to stay with yer women, knowin' that Keegan could get close enough to get what I needed."

"You knew they were watching her?" Asher asks from beside me, his voice coming out as lethal as my own.

"Aye. I did. They've been watchin' ye since ye brought her back. They were just waiting for their moment to take her, but I'm not as patient. I helped them move things along." Finn laughs. The fucker actually throws his head back and laughs at us.

"Kelsey was the fucking bait." My blood boils as I slam my fists down on his desk. Connor stands to his feet, but Finn waves him off.

"Did ye know they make these wee things smaller than the size of a button to help ye keep track of people? All me family has them now."

Every muscle in my body stills from that little confession. That sly son of a bitch. I can't stand the guy, but that is some impressive shit.

"I've got eyes everywhere, lad." The corners of his eyes crease as he smiles. He leans back in his leather chair, hands steepled out in front of him, flashing me a devil-may-care grin. "Let's go get me niece back. Shall we?"

35
KELSEY

"Hi, baby girl." My dad grunts and rolls against the cement floor.

"What have they done to you?" My heart lodges in my throat when I take in his appearance.

His usual well-groomed brown hair is a knotted mess. Two black eyes stand out against his green irises. There's a small cut on his cheek, and his bottom lip is split. Several bruises splatter along the side of his face, spilling onto his neck. He looks like something out of a horror movie.

"I'm fine." He pants as he pushes to his feet, propping himself up against the block wall. "They didn't hurt me much." I bury my head in my dad's chest and sob like I'm five years old again. He wraps me in his arms, patting my back. "It's going to be okay, baby girl."

"How can you say that? Look what they've done to you." I can't believe he's being so calm about all of this right now. "We have to get out of here."

"We'll be fine. They swore they wouldn't hurt us if we just gave them what they wanted. You still have it, don't you?" His hands shake as they grip the side of my face.

"Have what, Dad?" My mind races to make sense of what the hell he's talking about when his hold on my face tightens.

"The SD card, Kels." His voice grows hard as I take a good look at him. The man standing before me isn't my father. He's a stranger. The pupils of his eyes have gone black, and there's a far-off look in his eye that has my insides trembling. My mouth falls open as I stare down at the man. I've never seen him look so unhinged.

"Dad, what's wrong with you? Why are you acting like this?" I attempt to shake out of his hold, but his fingers dig into my cheeks even harder.

His hands fall away, and he starts pacing back and forth in the small space. He fists his hair, pulling at the tips, all the while mumbling to himself. I can only hear bits and pieces, but nothing that makes any sense. Something is seriously wrong with him. I don't recognize this man standing before me.

I plaster my body against the wall as the man who once taught me to ride a bike crumbles before my eyes. A lump forms in my throat taking it all in. It feels like I'm in a walking nightmare. Then he snaps and loses what little sanity he has left.

"Don't lie to me, you stupid bitch!" He shoves me to the floor and fists the side of his hair. "I gave it to you. You found it and hid it for yourself, didn't you? You selfish bitch." Spit flies from his mouth with every word.

"I didn't, I swear." Tears fill my eyes at the same time my heart shatters into a million pieces on the floor.

"You're fucking useless, just like your damn mother." He shoves me away from him with such force that I fall on my butt and smack my elbow against the cement, but I don't feel any of it. I'm too caught up in what he's just said.

"You bastard! You killed Mom, didn't you?"

He shrugs. "She got in my way."

I shake my head and press a hand against my stomach to settle the nausea churning inside me. My body rocks back and forth as I come to terms with the bomb he's just dropped on me. I can't believe any of this is happening.

My dad paces around the room for a couple of seconds, mumbling under his breath, before he stops and lifts his head up to glance over my shoulder. "I tried! What more do you want me to do?" I turn in time to see that lying bastard Murphy standing in the doorway with his arms crossed over his chest. I've been so lost in my own head that I never even heard him come in.

"I'm afraid that's not good enough." Murphy tilts his head to the side, studying my dad like he's a science experiment. "Ye know how this works, Frank. Our money or yer life—choice is yers."

"I already told you to take her. You can keep her for yourself or sell her to the highest bidder. It makes no difference to me. She's worth ten times what I owe you. You can have her, and you come out on top." The veins on the side of his neck pulse as he stares back at Murphy.

"Ye think I'm feckin' stupid, do ye?" Murphy's brown eyes narrow into tiny slits.

My dad's voice dips down an octave as he throws his hands up, placating him. "No. I don't. I'm just trying to help you out until I can get you your money."

"I'm takin' her anyway, and I don't need yer permission. She was mine the second ye fecked me over." Murphy pulls out a gun and waves it in our direction. A scream builds in my throat, but one look at the tightness in his face, and I zip my lips.

My dad isn't as smart. He charges at him at full speed like a damn bull. Murphy's ready for him, though. His finger squeezes the trigger before my dad can even make it a couple of steps. Blood soaks through the leg of his pants as he falls to the ground. I lose the battle then and scream my head off.

"You fucking shot me." My dad's hands put pressure on his leg, but blood seeps through his fingers.

"Aye, I did. Let's take a walk." Murphy steps back and gestures with the tip of his gun for me to step out of the room.

Without hesitation, I follow his orders. I'm smart enough to know when I'm outnumbered. It doesn't mean I won't get out of here—eventually. When I step through the doorway, he grabs me by the wrist and yanks me back against his chest.

Two guys are staring back at me with blank stares. One of them is the guy with the burns from earlier. They're both huge. They're not bulging with muscles like Axel or his brothers, but they still tower over me nonetheless.

"Take him upstairs and put him with the kid. I'll deal with them later." My spine stiffens at the mention of the kid. I know without a doubt that it's Teegan he's talking about. I'm relieved that he's alive but also scared shitless of what these bastards may have done to him.

"If you hurt Teegan, I'll—"

The hand on my arm moves to fist the back of my

hair and pull my head back until I'm staring up into a cold pair of brown eyes.

"Ye'll what? There's nothin' ye can do. So shut yer trap before I fill it with my dick and shut it for ye." Keeping a firm grip on my hair, he pushes my body forward. Faint grunts from my dad echo behind us as the two guys drag him along.

At the top of the stairs, we split up. They take my dad through a dark hallway off to the right. I go to follow them when I'm pulled back by my hair into Murphy's chest. "Yer with me." He shoves me in the opposite direction, through a house and up another set of stairs. Our steps never stop until we reach a bedroom.

Everything inside me trembles. Knowing what he has planned for me has my body in fight or flight mode. I claw at his hands until I feel pieces of his skin embedded underneath my nails and the wetness of his blood dripping down my fingers. My body never stops fighting. I've become the wildcat Axel always calls me. I fight against him with everything I have, but it's useless; he's too strong.

Murphy uses his weight to his advantage and shoves me forward until we're deep inside the room. With a quick shove of his hands, I'm tumbling face-first into the mattress. As soon as I land, I scramble up to my arms in a poor attempt to crawl away from him, but he's on me in a flash before I can even make it halfway across the bed and has me flipped over onto my back. The full weight of his body pins me down against the mattress. He bares his teeth at me as he wraps a hand around my throat.

"I've waited a long time for ye. And now yer mine." He trails the finger of his free hand down the side of my throat, stopping on my shirt. Without warning, he fists the cotton material and rips it down the middle. Cold air hits my skin as a lump forms in my throat. His gaze drops down to his exposed chest, and a wicked smile creeps onto his face. "I always knew ye were a lace girl."

"Fuck you, asshole! Axel will find me, and when he does, he's going to rip your dick off and make you choke on it." I make a fist and swing up, knocking him upside the head before he even has time to blink.

"Ye fecking cunt. Ye're going to regret that." Both hands come up to my neck and squeeze. His muscles are corded as red fills his face. "Dead or alive, I will feck ye. I don't mind sticking my dick in a corpse."

I kick my legs out to try and buck him off of me, but I can't get the upper hand no matter how hard I try. He's too heavy. Clawing at him only angers him further, and his hands clamp down even tighter. My lungs burn as the need for oxygen increases, and black spots cloud my vision. The more he deprives me of air, the more light-headed I become until I'm floating out of my body. I close my eyes and give myself over to the peaceful feeling coursing through me. This is the end. I feel it. I just hope Axel finds what's left of me before it's too late.

36
AXEL

The cherry of my cigarette glows against the night sky as we scope out the house from the van. It's out in the middle of nowhere with no one around for miles.

Each time one of those assholes walks the perimeter of the fence, my fists clench. There's nothing like being so close to her but still not able to rush in guns blazing to have me ready to fall off the ledge and fuck shit up. I shift in my seat, unable to contain myself.

Both of my brothers sit as still as stone on either side of me, smoking a cigarette, but I see the same storm brewing behind their eyes that matches my own. They enjoy watching and waiting for shit about as much as I do.

Rory plays with the tip of his Bowie knife but never takes his eyes off the house. Connor and Keegan are sitting next to him, looking just as focused while they load their Glocks. As much as I hate to think of her as one of them, I'm glad that Kelsey has these crazy bastards on her side.

A couple more vans full of Finn's guys wait in the same darkened area of the woods next to us. We're watching and waiting for something. For what, I have no fucking clue. I only know that Finn has a way of getting us in, and it involves Asher hacking the security system.

"How much longer? I sit here any longer and my ass is going to become dead weight." My fingers twitch with the need to break a few faces.

"Patience, lad. I want the same as ye. Me son is in there too, don't think I've forgotten that." Finn brushes off a fleck of imaginary dust from his suit and leans back against the leather seat.

"I'm not waiting out here all night." Zane pulls out his Glock and sends Finn a pointed look.

"Aye, but all the best hunters know that they catch the biggest game while lying in wait." Connor cocks his head to the side as he works something out in his head. "Just let your brother do what he needs to, and they're all ours."

"And trust me when we say they'll pay for touching any part of our family." Keegan nods his head as he cracks his knuckles.

"Just get us inside, and I'll find her. Y'all just handle the rest of these pricks so I can get her out in one piece." I've sat on the sidelines long enough with the what-ifs running through my mind, and my stomach is filled with cement as I think of what they could be doing to her.

"I'm in. Get out of the car and stick to the west side of the house. The cameras will be disabled when the power's cut, but he's got a backup generator that'll kick in five minutes after that. That's the only window we have to sneak in undetected."

"Good." Finn glances at his watch and lifts the corner of his mouth in a grin. "Ye lads remember the plan?"

A round of agreements comes spewing out from all six of us, and Finn nods his head. Connor hands each of us a pair of night vision goggles before we exit out of the van into the cold night air.

Asher hands Finn the laptop and tells him what to do with the cameras, then follows us outside. Before he can close the door, Finn holds up his hand to stop us. "Remember one thing, lads—her da is mine." The pained look in his eye tells me all I need to know. He wants payback for his sister. I can respect him for that, and I will make sure it happens.

"You got it." I nod and follow after the guys, taking small steps and hiding behind trees as we encroach further onto the house.

One of the guards watching the perimeter is mere inches from us taking a piss, facing the opposite direction as us. Rory takes full advantage and creeps up behind him, slicing his knife across his throat in one quick motion. The guard doesn't even have a chance to realize what hit him before he's down and bleeding out on the cold ground with his flaccid dick out for all to see. I have to admit Rory is starting to grow on me.

"I like you, Irish. You're one crazy motherfucker." I jerk my chin out as I take in his handiwork. It's clean, neat, and efficient.

"Same, Country." Rory nods and peers around the corner before he motions us further forward until we're standing right outside the gate.

"How long do we have to wait here, Ash?" I ask.

"Not long. Should be in three, two, one." No sooner does Asher get out the one than everything goes black. "That's our cue," Asher says, and all of us slip the goggles over our eyes.

We slip in through the side gate, unnoticed, as we hear a commotion of voices coming from the front of the house. Rory leads the way, slicing the throat of anyone who gets in our way.

My blood pumps in my veins like a wildfire as we make our way through the back door and into the side of the house. Each step I take has my adrenaline spiking. A pained grunt comes from off to the side at the same time a scream rings out from upstairs. Without a second thought, I haul ass up there as the other guys head off in the direction of the grunting. My steps are light as I listen to each one of the closed doors until I stop at the right one. The second I hear Kelsey's cries, I shove my boot through the door, splintering the wood. What I find has me ready to string this fucker up by his balls.

Kelsey's on the bed, bra exposed, and unconscious with a blonde prick on top of her. Being in the dark with my goggles gives me the advantage I need, and I manage to catch him before he can get away.

"You're dead, motherfucker." I race into the room and knock the puka shell-wearing fuck to the floor.

"What the feck?"

We roll around on the floor, swinging our fists at anything we can. During the struggle, he's able to grab the collar of my shirt and tries to punch me in the face. I jerk out of his grip just in time and use the weight of my lower body to roll him under me. My fist clenches, ready to break his nose, but before I can, I'm blinded by an explosion of light.

The generators have clicked back on, giving him the upper hand. He manages to get a couple of hits in before he kicks me in the stomach and knocks the wind out of me. I rip the goggles off and let my eyes take a second to adjust to the light, then all bets are off.

"You fucked with the wrong girl."

"I did. Her cunt is so fucking tight. I can't wait to have another go." He licks his bottom lip, taunting me.

My vision goes black as the words leave his mouth. I've seen Asher do it, but I've never experienced it myself until now. Hit after hit, I don't let up. His blood coats my hands, and I thrive on it.

"Axel!" It takes a minute for Zane's voice to register, and when it does, the spell that I was under has been broken. "He's passed out."

"We'll take him out of here. You take care of Kelsey." Asher's on my other side, holding my stare. There's no judgment on his face, but then again I knew there wouldn't be. He's done the same thing, even worse, himself for Charlee.

"Make sure he's left for me."

"We will, little brother." The darkness in Asher's eyes matches my own at the moment. I nod but don't watch them drag his limp ass out of the room. My mind is on much more important things.

I whip off my shirt and cover her with it. My hands slip under her body, doing my best to ignore the bruises forming on her face and around her neck. I cradle her tight against my chest like she's a newborn and inhale her familiar scent of mango that's almost overpowered by that ass clown's smell. Once she's secure in my arms,

I carry her out of there. Never stopping until we reach the van, where Finn awaits.

He cracks his neck from side to side and clenches his jaw. "They will both pay for this."

I nod but don't say anything else. Nothing needs to be said. I got what I came for. The only question left is when will Kelsey wake up.

37
AXEL

My fingers twitch with anticipation. I've been ready to have a go at this fucker since we got Kelsey back. Asher and Zane are both quiet as they walk behind me. Adrenaline's still strumming through their veins much like mine is at the moment.

"How's Kelsey?" Connor asks from beside his brother Rory.

"She's upstairs and still hasn't woken up. How's Teegan?"

"A little banged up, but he'll be fine." Connor's face hardens at thoughts of what those pricks did to his little brother, and he can't say I blame him.

"Don't you worry about it. My dad had his doctor check them out, and he's the best you'll find this side of the Chattanooga River." Keegan slaps me on the back and runs ahead of us into the first set of doors.

I take in the block walls and cement floors that lead to two smaller rooms that each have their own door. There's even a drain in the center of the floor for easy cleanup. Finn has one hell of a "working space" under-neath his house, complete with soundproof walls. I wasn't sure what to expect when we came down here, but it wasn't this.

"Right." That's the only reason I'm down here and not glued to her side.

Connor and Rory follow Keegan into the room directly ahead of us. The closer I get to the open door, the better my view becomes. Kelsey's dad is strung up from the ceiling like a piñata. The gunshot wound in his leg has been half-ass taken care of. No sense in wasting good care on someone who's bound to die anyway.

"Been a long time, Frank." Finn shoots me a wink as Keegan closes the door. I return his gesture with a small jerk of my chin. That has to be one hell of a family reunion happening in there. With the soundtrack of Frank's screams hitting my ears, I head into the room next door for some justice of my own, with my brothers following in right after me.

The puka shell-wearing fucker is strapped to a metal table in the middle of the room, tied up neatly like a Christmas present. His bloodshot eyes watch my every move—waiting, wondering when I'll strike, and this is when the game becomes as easy as breathing for me.

"How's it going?" I tilt my head to the side, enjoying the sight of him like this a little too much. Shit like this really gets my blood pumping.

The piece of shit's face hardens, and that's the only tell I need to know my words are having the intended impact. He's not going to make this easy on himself by any means, but that makes this all that much sweeter for me.

Zane hands me a pair of pruning shears.

"Interesting choice, Z." I arch an eyebrow at him, but he shrugs it off and goes back to messing with that knot of hair on top of his head. I swear he needs to just cut that shit off already.

Asher stays silent in the corner of the room as he watches me do what I need to do.

I open and close the shears, enjoying the way Puka Shell jumps at the sound of metal grinding together that slices through the air.

"Which finger?"

"What?" His blonde eyebrows shoot up to his forehead. The look on his face would be comical if I wasn't in the mood to fuck his face up.

"You took my woman. Hurt her and violated her." I wag a finger at him like I'm scolding a dog for shitting on the carpet. "So, I will ask you again. Which. Finger?"

"Aye. I can still taste her pussy on me tongue. She tastes like berries and cream." He licks his lips as he spews his word vomit.

Red fills my vision. He just lit the match and detonated my fuse. Without a second thought, I slice the pruning shears through all four of his fingers at the same time. He cries like a little bitch, but his pleas fall on deaf ears. I repeat the same move on his other hand, earning me another tirade of screams.

Once I'm finished, I step back and admire my handiwork. Blood pours out the stumps where his fingers used to be as he wiggles his thumbs that are still attached. "Would y'all look at that? Fucker is all thumbs now." His eyes start to droop closed, and that won't do for what I have planned. "Hey, don't pass out on me. We're just getting started." I slap his cheeks a couple of times until his eyes open back up.

"Now, normally I would take my time and cut off each finger one by one until you're about to pass out from the pain or die from blood loss, but my Wildcat needs me more." My lips curl in a smile that doesn't reach my eyes. "Mercy isn't a word I know when it comes to scum like you."

"Go to hell!"

"You first. And when you get there, you be sure to tell the devil the Savage brothers send their regards." I bring the shears up, ready to start in on this asshole's toes, when Asher stops me.

"Why don't you go upstairs and check on Kelsey? Z and I would like to have a little fun with this piece of shit." A muscle in Asher's jaw jerks when he glances in the direction of the table. He needs a piece of this too. The bastard may not have taken Charlee or Lily, but he scared them, and to Asher, that's just as bad.

"Okay, big brother." I hand him the pruning shears and stare back at the table one more time. A part of me wants to stay and continue this, but another part is itching to get out of here and up to the room where Kelsey is. Without a backward glance, I walk out of the room. "I'm going to see my woman. You two play nice, now." I curl my lips into a wide smile and whistle the whole way down the hall and up the stairs, knowing he'll be getting exactly what he deserves. And as much as I would like to spend hours down here torturing him, I've been away from my girl long enough.

38
KELSEY

A filter of colors swirls in front of me until my
eyes adjust to the light. My throat is tender to
the touch. It feels like I've swallowed broken
glass. I tilt my head to take in the strange bedroom but
let out a sharp groan. Everything hurts.

"Easy there, Wildcat. I've got you." A warm finger
strokes the side of my head, and he leans over until I'm
staring up at my favorite pair of blue eyes.

"Ax?"

Dark circles mar his features as he rubs his thumb
along my upper lip. "You took years off my life tonight."

"I'm sorry."

"Don't you dare say you're sorry. This wasn't your
fault. It was mine for not protecting you." The muscles
of his throat flex as he swallows.

Overcome with the need to touch him, I try to sit up.
That's a huge mistake. My body is one giant ball of pain
that knocks the wind out of me and has me falling back
against the mattress with a soft whimper.

"Careful." Warm hands press my shoulders back

down against the mattress. "Finn had his doctor check you out to make sure you're okay, but I still don't want you to risk it." He shifts his weight to stand, and a wave of anxiety courses through me.

"Will you stay with me?" My hands turn clammy at the thought of him leaving me here alone.

"I'm not going anywhere." He pulls me into his chest and intertwines our bodies together. "Wildcat, I need to know something." His thumbs draw small circles along the sides of my cheeks as I see a storm building behind his baby blues. "I need to know if he—" He clears his throat a couple of times and forces out the rest of his words after a couple of tries. "Did he touch you?"

"No. You got to me in time before he could..." I can't bring myself to finish those words, but Axel understands without me having to do so.

His shoulders sag next to me as he lets out the breath I didn't realize he was holding at my answer. "Thank Christ." He lies back on the bed and pulls me in tight against his side as his hand rubs along my back. No words are spoken, but none are needed. Axel knows what I need without me having to tell him.

"It's okay. You're safe, and I've got you. I always will, Wildcat," he whispers against the top of my head.

"Knock. Knock." Charlee's voice cuts through our silent haven.

Axel lets out a deep sigh that I feel against my head. "I could have sworn I locked the damn door."

"You did." She shrugs and steps into the room, bouncing a happy Lily on her hip. "Asher's been teaching me how to pick them." She motions to him as he trails into the room behind her.

Axel sits up against the headboard and pulls me up

next to him. "Man, you need to control your woman." Axel cocks his head to the side and shoots his older brother a pointed stare.

Asher's lips twitch into a sliver of a smile, which for him is huge, but he doesn't comment otherwise. Instead, his gaze lands on me. "How are you feeling, Kelsey?"

"I've been better."

"Where's Z?" Axel asks as he glances around the room.

"Around," is all Asher says, but that word means much more to Axel because a huge grin spreads across his face, showcasing his dimples.

"Thatta boy, Z." Axel's comment is met with silence. It's clear there's something more going on, and when I'm feeling back to normal, I'm going to get it out of them. Every detail.

Lily chooses that moment to make her presence known. "Someone else has missed you and wants to say hi." Charlee laughs and hands me the squirming baby.

"Hey, little one." I stare down at those wide green eyes, and my heart melts. Drool drips down her chubby cheeks as she gnaws on her fist.

Axel leans in until I can feel the heat of his breath against the nape of my neck. "You look hot as fuck like this, and I can't wait to put my babies in you." He presses a quick kiss to my neck and starts playing with Lily's hand like he didn't just drop a bomb on me.

My heart hammers in my chest as I picture dark-haired little ones running around with their dad's blue eyes and dimples. The thought has my thighs pressing together.

Lily giggles and wipes a sticky hand on Axel's face.

"Thanks for that, Wildflower." He cringes and wipes at his face when the sound of a throat clearing has all of our attention.

"Ye're awake." A man in a suit that resembles a 1920s gangster smiles at me from the doorway.

My eyebrows pinch together as I shoot a look Axel's way. A muscle in his jaw tics underneath my stare. "Kelsey, this is—"

"Yer Uncle Finn." The man from the door smiles, causing the corners of his blue eyes to crease. He's taking great joy in Axel's discomfort.

"Thank you for everything." Unsure of what else to do, I press my lips together and offer him a small smile. He may be my mother's brother, but it's going to take me some time to feel comfortable around him.

"It was nothin'. Yer family, and we protect our own. Nothin' like that will happen to ye ever again. Ye have me word." Finn dips his chin and strolls out of the room just as silently as he appeared.

"I know he's your uncle and everything, Wildcat, but he scares the shit out of even me, and I live with this fucker's ugly face." Axel jabs a thumb in Asher's direction.

"Fuck off, Ax." Asher shakes his head, but there's no harshness to his words.

Taking in every person that's in this room and watching these two battle it out has a warmth spreading across my chest. For so long, I've felt lost and alone, like I had no one. I may have lost both of my parents, but now I've found something better, something that makes me feel complete—a family.

EPILOGUE
AXEL

FOUR WEEKS LATER...

"Come on, Ax. You afraid of a little rematch?" Kelsey bats those baby blues at me at the same time she purses her plump lips—lips that were wrapped around my dick hours ago. She leans her hip against the side of the pool table as a few fallen red curls frame her face. Everything she does is hot as fuck.

"You sure you're ready to lose again?" I cock my head to the side and take another swig of my Budweiser. My eyes travel down her green top, admiring the way it pushes out her tits, but it's the skin-tight jeans molding against her curves that has my dick weeping in joy.

"Last time didn't count." Her auburn eyebrows pinch together as she taps the heels of her new brown boots together. Those were the first purchases we made when she felt well enough to leave Finn's place. She needed new boots for new memories. A smile flashes across my face as I recall fucking her from behind in the kitchen the day she got them as she wore nothing else but them. "We had distractions."

"Right." I know a losing battle when I hear one and let it go. Truth is I could spend eternity arguing with her when she gets all flushed like that, but I have another motive. "Then we need us a little wager." I wiggle my eyebrows at her.

"What did you have in mind?" Her tongue darts out to lick her lip as she swallows. Oh yeah. My Wildcat is turned on.

"If I win, I get to tap your ass." Color flushes her cheeks at the mention of me getting anywhere near her back door, and it's cute as fuck.

"And if I win?" She crosses her arms over her chest and waits me out.

"Whatever you want, Wildcat."

"Those are your terms?" She cocks her head to the side and studies me. I have a slight feeling I may have screwed myself, but if it means finally getting inside her sweet ass, it's worth it.

"Yup."

Something works behind her eyes a beat before her lips curl into a smile and she nods her head. "You're on, Savage."

"You going to tell me what I have to do if I lose?"

"Nope, I like the element of surprise. All I will say is you have a sweet ride." Her lips pop on the P, accentuating the sound and making my balls tingle, but then the last half of her words catch up to my brain.

"No way." I slice my hands through the air as I shake my head. "Asher just bought me that. There is no way I'm letting anyone but me touch her."

"Oh, I ain't gonna touch. I get to name her." Damn

woman is evil. She has me by the dick and she knows it, but never underestimate a man and his need for ass.

"Fine." I glance over at Zane and shake my head. Fucker's been sulking all damn night. I wish Asher and Charlee would have come out, but Asher's been pretty busy trying to give Lily a sibling.

"Order another beer. We'll be quick." I don't wait for Zane's response before I'm out of my seat and on a mission. Lucky for me, the pool tables are right next to our table. I stick some coins into the slot and smirk as the balls clank together. "Rack 'em, Wildcat."

"You got it, Mr. Savage." Her voice dips an octave, vibrating across my skin like honey.

"Oh, I like that. I'm going to have you call me that when I'm balls deep in your ass later." I moisten my bottom lip with my tongue, showing just what she's in store for tonight.

"We shall see." Her ass bends over in those tight-as-fuck jeans, sending all the blood straight to my dick. She works the pool stick between her fingers in small, seductive strokes, causing the pressure in my balls to ache. Little tease.

From the time she sinks the first ball, the game is a close one. Kelsey takes any opportunity to flash me her ass when she can in hopes that it'll distract me. Little does she know that I can multitask like a motherfucker. Doesn't mean I don't enjoy the show.

Round for round, we go until we're down to the eight ball. I align my shot and blow her a kiss. "Don't forget the lube tonight, Wildcat."

She shakes her head but doesn't contest it. Interesting.

I slide the stick back, ready to take the final shot,

when four angry-looking Irish brothers come barreling through the crowd.

"I'm going to bloody kill you!" Rory shouts as Connor lunges forward. The twins stay back like the two little guard pups they are.

Before I have time to blink, Connor swings his fist into Zane's face, hitting him square on the nose.

Zane falls back out of his chair, which knocks my arm forward, and my stick clips the side of the cue ball. It shoots straight down the table to the last pocket, missing the damn eight ball.

Kelsey throws her arms up in the air as she lets out a throaty laugh. "Scratch! I win."

"No way. That was a cheap shot." I set the stick down, ready to kick some Irish ass, when Zane gets to his feet.

"What the fuck was that for?" He wipes at the blood dripping from his nose with the side of his hand, glaring at the Donnelly boys. His hair falling around his face.

Connor's nostrils flare as he jabs a finger in Zane's face. "You knocked up our sister."

A LOOK AT BOOK THREE
RUTHLESS

They broke me once. Now I'll break everything to protect her.

For eight years, I've lived with the ghosts—silent, screaming, always there. I tried to forget. Tried to move on. But the past doesn't die—it waits.

Kennedy Donnelly was never part of the plan. The Irish princess. Off-limits. Untouchable. One night with her changed everything, and now she's caught in the crossfire.

They came for her. They'll regret it.

Because when they touched her, they woke something in me I've spent years trying to bury. Ruthless is what I have to be to save her. To save *us*. And I won't stop until the whole damn world knows it.

AVAILABLE DECEMBER 2025

ACKNOWLEDGMENTS

There are so many people I need to thank for helping me make it to the finish line with this book. Some days it was really a struggle to get the words out, and without the support of my crazy crew I wouldn't have gotten this far.

First up, I have to thank my Z. Without you I'd be lost. You support me and my writing, whether it's by being my sounding board or attending signings and becoming one of the girls for the weekend. Thank you for putting up with all of my chaos and loving me through it all.

Thank you so much to my girls, Lisa and Christy. You put up with listening to me bitch and moan about my self-doubt and writer's block like the badass friend you are. You two are my rocks as I do my best not to drown some days, and I love your faces so much for it. My betas—Evelyn, Christina, Michelle, Naomi, Tre, and Shelby—thank you so much for all of your feedback. I'd be lost without you. To all of the bloggers who took the time to share and read my words, y'all are loved and appreciated more than you know. To my editor, Heather, thank you for always making sure my grammar is spot-on and holding nothing back. (Obviously, she hasn't seen this page.)

And lastly, I need to do a big shout-out to you, the reader. Thank you. Thank you. Thank you. Without you, the voices in my head would remain just that. You were brave enough to take a chance on my crazy world, and for that, I am forever grateful. I hope you enjoyed reading about these characters as much as I enjoyed writing them.

I'm going to take a deep breath before diving back into the darkness. Next up is Zane and Kennedy's story, and I'm going to need more vodka to survive this.

Christine Besze is a writer, reader, mother, wife, and lover of all things wine. She lives in her own world of crazy most days, because the voices inside her head hold some great conversation. When she does have to come back to reality and act like an actual grown-up, she spends her time with her handsome hubby Z, their two gorgeous gingers and their mini-herd of German Shepherds. Born in sunny Southern California, she now lives with her family on the East Coast and couldn't be happier. You'll still find her in flip-flops—with a full glass of wine—all year round.

www.christinebesze.net